In Too Deep

Book 2, The Liliana Series

by

Neva Squires-Rodriguez

Vanilla Heart Publishing

In Too Deep
Book 2, The Liliana Series
by Neva Squires-Rodriguez

Copyright 2014 Neva Squires-Rodriguez

Published by: Vanilla Heart Publishing
www.VanillaHeartBookAndAuthors.com
10121 Evergreen Way, 25-156
Everett, WA 98204 USA

ISBN-13: 978-0692348437   ISBN-10: 0692348433

10 9 8 7 6 5 4 3 2 1 First Edition

First Printing, December 2014
Printed in the United States of America

In Too Deep

Book 2, The Liliana Series

by

Neva Squires-Rodriguez

Table of Contents

Dedication

Prologue... pg 13
Chapter One... pg 17
Chapter Two... pg 37
Chapter Three... pg 53
Chapter Four... pg 75
Chapter Five... pg 93
Chapter Six... pg 113
Chapter Seven... pg 133
Chapter Eight... pg 143
Chapter Nine... pg 161

Book Club Discussion Starters

More Great Books by Neva Squires-Rodriguez

Author Bio, Photo, and Contact Info

Dedication

I would first like to thank God for allowing me a chance to make it into print for a second time, third if you count my Christmas short story of faith. Each book is considered a blessing to me, which I am extremely thankful for.

Secondly, I would like to thank all my family and friends in helping "Liliana" be so successful over social media by sharing links to the book. My mother of course, my husband Cecilio, my cousin Allison, my friends Chelle, Charmaine, Divya, Jasmine, Kimm, Lauren, Linda, Marilyn, Mewsette, Milagro, Rebecca, Tamara, Tiffany and so many of my Twitter friends that I do not personally know. Thank you also to all the sites that allow me to post to their group pages, retweet my postings and even those who have written on my books from other websites that are new to me, to Glen Flora Dental in Waukegan, Illinois for putting my book on display and to the many book clubs who have picked the book up to read as a part of their organization. I can't tell you all how much I appreciate all of you. Without you, I wouldn't be sharing In Too Deep with you and with the rest of the world. I would also like to thank everyone who rated Liliana on Amazon and Goodreads I can't tell you how much I appreciate the great ratings. Let's keep them coming!

Finally, I would like to thank my publisher, Vanilla Heart Publishing for seeing a vision in my original query letter and for asking for more. It is incredibly difficult when you are the new fish in the water and I thank VHP for taking me under their wing. We may not be the biggest, or best paid in the business, but we definitely are the closest publishing group in the business and it is good to know that when I send Kimberlee "K'lee" Williams an email, she knows who I am.

May God be good to all of us. My prayers to each one of you whether you are reading my book online or holding that beautiful paper copy in your hands.

Prologue

Our wedding night had been a whirlwind of noise and celebration, and I awoke early the morning after, with a headache. Sunlight beamed in through the white lace curtains. Antonio was not beside me and the sheets were thrown to the side where he had been sleeping. I wondered if he was in the bathroom but after five minutes or so I realized that the bathroom door was open and there were no noises coming from inside.

I was completely naked but lay there without moving until I saw a white silk robe on a chair nearby. I put it on and luckily I did, because moments later the door opened. The maid came in slowly with a tray of breakfast, glancing around the room as she did. As our eyes met, she quickly left and I began to eat.

Elena came in shortly after. "Are you okay?" She asked, smiling at me coyly.

I rubbed my body and nodded.

"I can't believe that you let my mother do that." She motioned to the balcony and I walked over to it seeing a sheet flailing around in the wind with blood spots on it.

I quickly took it down and rolled it up in a ball, throwing it in the garbage can in disgust.

"Oh no." I exclaimed, holding my hand to my face. "How embarrassing! I didn't realize that happened."

"You didn't know that she did that?" Elena asked.

I shook my head. I sat down and continued to eat my food slowly, without saying a word. What was I supposed to say? Whatever was done was done.

"Where is he?" I asked, I finally asked her.

"Where else?" Elena responded. "At a meeting, where else?"

I sat in frustration for a moment without knowing what to say. I thought Antonio would have stayed here with me. I thought that he would stay with me today or the rest of the week. I shook bad thoughts from my mind as I sat back.

Elena began to talk about the reception. She had taken some pictures on her cell phone and I looked through them without remembering taking as many pictures as I had. I must have walked off with her at some part of the night because she had pictures of me posing in different parts of the banquet hall for her with people that I didn't remember. I hadn't realized that I was that drunk until now.

Antonio came in moments later and shooed Elena out of the room. He quickly came to my side and kissed me. He pulled the sash on my robe and before I knew it, we started going at it again. He didn't give me a chance to question him as he thrust himself inside me. I moaned loudly in pleasure and he smiled, leaning down to suck on my neck.

"I want a son." He whispered to me. "Give me a son."

He bit down lightly on my neck again, moaning. I felt a blast of warmth inside me and he paused before falling to the side. I tried to get up, thinking I needed to take a shower, but he pulled me back down and made love to me again. My insides throbbed in pain as he penetrated me for what felt like hours. My legs felt like they locked to either side of me and it hurt to switch positions as he moved me all over the bed.

While he was inside of me, we didn't talk, I just moaned and grabbed onto his back, as he thrust himself into me. He would smile fiercely with each moan that escaped me. He bit down on my skin from time to time, causing me to moan louder in both ecstasy and

14

pain. Sweat dripped from his body onto me and glistened as it fell across his muscular arms. His chest boasted the perfect amount of hair, just across the middle and top but very thin. I touched it as he made love to me, glancing up at him to take in his expression.

Over the next two months, every moment we spent together went like this. I had little time to eat or to shower when he was around so I tried to get all of my own personal things done while he was at his morning meetings. He wore my body out, making love to me for hours upon hours each day. If I went to the bathroom to try to take a quick shower, he would appear from nowhere and pull my legs around him, holding me in a standing position as he pounded himself powerfully into me and pressed me against the shower wall.

I never fought him off or pushed him away. Soon it wasn't just Antonio that initiated our lovemaking. It got to the point where as soon as he came in the bedroom door, I was the one attacking him with passionate kisses and guiding him to the bed where he would begin to penetrate me.

He'd told me the day after we were married that he didn't want me to leave the room or even to get dressed until I was carrying his baby, and I played along with him. He wanted me to be there, ready for him, and those were the rules. I thought of it as a game at first but after a month or so, I was starting to feel like his prisoner.

When Antonio wasn't there, I began to feel sad and lonely. Elena stopped coming over as much because Antonio wanted me all to himself when he was home. I told him that I felt like I was being held captive in many ways. He wouldn't listen to me when I tried to talk to him about how I felt. It got to the point that I thought that I might never see the outside world again. I was dependent on him to bring me everything and while I enjoyed living my new luxurious life, I didn't like it at all, at the same time.

After a few weeks feeling sad about it, I became lost in our passionate love affair, living and breathing solely for his touch. It got to the point where he was all I lived for... maybe that was his goal all along.

Chapter One

Finally, one Saturday morning, we realized that all of Antonio and my dreams had come true. I woke up earlier than usual feeling nauseous and dizzy. I tapped Antonio's shoulder, belched and then staggered into the bathroom. I felt like I had to throw up, but nothing would come out as I gagged relentlessly standing over the bathroom sink. I went to lie back down beside Antonio after the feeling stopped.

Antonio immediately noticed something was wrong. He sat up in bed and stared intently at me. "What's wrong?" He asked, touching my shoulder gently.

I shrugged as I lay beside him. Antonio called for the maid and moments later she brought breakfast up.

"¿Estás bien?" She asked me, as her eyes studied my face. "Ella se ve pálida."

Antonio said something to her that I didn't catch and she came over to the side of the bed and put her hand on my forehead, shaking her head and looking confused as she slowly pulled away. Antonio thanked her and she left our room. I got up and walked to the balcony and lowered myself into a patio chair, figuring the fresh air would help me. The sun was just rising and I could see the sunlight glistening on the blades of grass in our yard.

Antonio carried the tray of food out to the balcony and we sat down to eat. I smiled up at him as he put the tray down in front of me. No sooner did I see the eggs on my plate then I turned to my side and vomited. Antonio quickly rushed over to my side and rubbed my back. I wiped my face with my napkin, feeling as though I had turned green. My first instinct was to run to the bathroom, but my body suddenly felt so weak that I didn't think I could move.

"Baby, are you okay?" He asked worriedly.

I shook my head, though I couldn't talk. I still felt like vomiting and did several times off the side of the balcony as he watched with a disgusted look on his face. He came over after the second time to hold my hair and rub my back as I vomited acid out of the depths of my stomach. I grabbed onto him after the vomiting fit ceased and he helped me sit back down in the chair. I wiped sweat from my forehead as a smile appeared on his face.

"Lily, your monthly friend hasn't visited at all since we've been married." Antonio exclaimed suddenly.

I sat in shock for a moment as I thought about it.

"No." I replied. "Actually it hasn't."

No sooner did I confirm what he had said, than Antonio had a smile on his face from ear to ear. He picked me up and carried me to the bed.

"I'm going to be a papa!" He exclaimed.

"Quiet. Please Tony, don't get excited yet." I said quietly. "I mean we don't know for sure."

"No." He replied loudly. "I know for sure. I have a feeling about this. I'm calling the doctor."

He picked up his cell phone and called his mother for the doctor's number and avoided her questions, saying that he would call her back later. He quickly dialed the doctor and ordered him to come over immediately, saying that he didn't care how much it cost him. A second later he ran out onto the balcony.

"I'm going to be a papa." He screamed, leaning over the side, looking like he would lose his balance and fall.

"Oh my goodness." I said putting my hand over my face, blushing.

One of the gardeners shouted out his congratulations to Antonio as they talked back and forth.

Minutes later, the doctor pulled into the driveway and Antonio ran out of the room and down the stairs to bring him up to our room.

Antonio pushed the doctor along as he entered our room with him moments later. Antonio stayed in the room while the doctor examined me, becoming nervous as the doctor took his time to give him his opinion.

"Congratulations." The doctor said, confirming the answer that Antonio had been waiting for. "She is about six weeks along."

Antonio immediately jumped up and hugged him. I smiled as I watched Antonio. He looked as though he had received the best news in the world. I was excited, but I thought Antonio was much more excited than I was. I asked him not to tell anyone that I was pregnant until I was at least halfway through the pregnancy.

"Why?" He asked, with a childish look on his face.

"I don't know." I replied. "I'm just nervous, I guess."

I felt kind of embarrassed, I knew everyone knew that we were married, but now they would know that we had sex. I just wasn't used to talking about things like that. I remembered when I had my first period, I didn't even tell my mother about it, she found out on her own a week later when she was doing the laundry. I was only eleven and she had been planning to talk to me about menstruation when I was twelve, thinking that I wouldn't have my first period until I was thirteen like she did.

Antonio paced the room but paid little attention to me as he called his mother to tell her to have everyone come to the house for a barbeque that afternoon. I sighed, knowing that he would not be able to contain the news and asked him if I could have my clothes back. He took me across the hall to another bedroom where all of our clothes were in the closet. This room had a larger bathroom and its balcony overlooked the backyard. He told me we would stay in that room from that point on in our marriage as he happily showed me where everything was.

The room boasted deep colors of brown and red. The sheets on the bed felt silky and smooth as I ran my hand down them. I grabbed him and tried to pull him close to me for a kiss, but he pulled my hand and led me out to the balcony where he had the maid bring up some crackers and ginger ale for me. Antonio and I sat out on the balcony for a few hours letting everything sink in before realizing that we had to get ready for the barbeque.

"Everyone should be here soon." He said. "Do you need help getting ready?"

I shook my head and got up slowly, going inside and removing my robe he watched me. I took a hot shower as he stood at a distance, handing me soap and shampoo so that I wouldn't have to bend down to lift it up. He held out a towel for me, drying me up as I came out. I put on comfortable clothing and my stomach clenched as I reached down to put on my gym shoes.

"Do you need me to tie your shoes?" He asked.

"No, Tony. I'm fine." I replied.

His excitement was getting me excited. I did feel like I needed a few minutes to myself, to let the baby news sink in. When he began getting ready, I took the opportunity to think about what was going on. I felt the shock sinking in. I couldn't believe that I had a baby growing inside of me. I rubbed my stomach, as I thought about it. Antonio noticed and came to my side and hugged me.

"My baby's having my baby." He said.

I closed my eyes in an attempt to cherish the memory forever. This was the happiest moment of my life. I felt happier than the day that we were married, or the day that I had met him. I had always wondered what it would be like to become a mother. Soon, I would know.

I leaned against him and he put his hand on my stomach as we sat down on the bed. He laid me back on the bed slowly and kissed my stomach lightly. He hugged me and then lightly began to move his fingers through my hair. I closed my eyes and he kissed my eyelids.

"Are you tired baby?" He asked, and stroked my eyelids softly until I fell asleep.

After what felt like only a few minutes, the doorbell rang. Antonio got up quietly, and left the room. I slowly rolled to my side and got out of bed. I put on a little makeup and then walked slowly downstairs. As I walked down the stairs I noticed that Antonio was handing out cigars to our guests.

They smiled up at me, and Antonio came to my side to help me.

"Here she is." Antonio exclaimed. "My beautiful wife and my child in waiting."

Everyone cheered again and began coming over to hug me and kiss my cheek. I must have turned beet red, I was so embarrassed.

"I know you didn't want me to say anything, Lily." Antonio called out, "but I couldn't help it."

"Aye, you're going to be a papa, mijo!" Marcus said as he put his arm around Antonio's shoulder and led him outside.

Roberta quickly came and began asking me questions about my pregnancy. I spoke with her as Blanca glanced at us from across the room with an expression that made me question how she felt about the pregnancy.

Minutes later Antonio was back at my side. He went out of his way to make me comfortable. He even insisted on feeding me steak tacos and rice by hand. I was hoping that he would calm down about the pregnancy, but as the day progressed he didn't. Blanca even yelled at him and told him that he was smothering me as he patted my face down with a napkin after seeing me miss my mouth with my cup.

"Shut up woman." He replied to her jokingly.

Blanca didn't look like she took the joke well and ended up avoiding me the rest of the night. Elena couldn't stop smiling at me. She told me how excited she was at the thought of becoming an aunt. I had begun to become excited about the pregnancy after everyone left.

Antonio and I curled up in bed as soon as the last guest had left and we talked about the excitement that we were both feeling. We talked for at least ten minutes, before I decided to climb on him and kiss him. He pushed me back immediately and turned on the television.

"Let's watch a movie," was his response.

"Okay." I said laughing, thinking he was joking and began kissing his neck.

He pushed me away again, this time roughly and I became upset.

"What's wrong?" I asked as I wiped loose strands of hair from my face. I wasn't used to getting this kind of a reaction from him. Every night since we'd been married, we had taken advantage of our marriage, kissing and making love all night long. Tonight he wanted to watch television. I didn't get it.

"I can't make love to you." He said apologetically. "Now I know that my baby is in there." He began to rub my stomach and smile.

I folded my arms across my chest and stared angrily at him. He turned back to the television and used the remote to begin flipping channels as I sat up straight on the bed. Was this how it was going to be? I wondered. I stared at him as my nostrils flared heavily.

"It didn't stop you last night." I retorted after a moment.

"I didn't know last night." He replied, without looking at me.

I leaned back against the pillows and sulked. Would he be like this during my whole pregnancy I wondered? I felt extremely sad. I sat there as he watched television intently and suddenly I felt unattractive. A tear ran down the left side of my face as I sat staring blankly at the television. I noticed several tattoos on his back that I had never seen before and questioned him about them. He sighed and turned to me, kissing me on the side of my wet cheek.

"Lily, I'm tired." He said to me. "Can we go to sleep?"

He reached over me and turned off the light, without waiting for an answer.

I lay there in shock for a while. What had just happened? I felt completely rejected. He didn't even try to hold me as we attempted to go to sleep. When I finally relaxed a little, he reached over and began to rub my stomach again. I felt animosity grow toward him until I fell asleep.

The next morning he had to go to a meeting and kissed me on the cheek before running out the door of our room. This was not my first morning having breakfast alone, but suddenly I felt more alone than ever. I played with my food for a while and drank my orange juice. Everything looked disgusting to me. I knew that I wouldn't be able to keep it down so I didn't even try to eat it. A couple minutes later the juice came up.

I ran to the bathroom and vomited again and again into the to the white toilet bowl. I swished water around in my mouth and tried to regain my composure. I felt horrible. I finally had my clothes and could walk all over the house and all that I wanted to do was fall over and lay down in the bed. I called up Elena as I did just that and told her how I was feeling. I cried into the phone and within an hour she came over with her son. Elena rubbed a cool cloth on my head as I moaned.

"What's wrong with me Elena?" I moaned. "I feel so horrible. Is this normal?"

"Every pregnancy is different." She said to me. "I never felt that badly, but it doesn't mean that it's not normal."

She stayed with me the rest of the day. Antonio came home in the afternoon and then left again after seeing that she was caring for me. He didn't return until later that night after it was dark and everyone had left. I was too tired to ask him where he had been. He didn't offer an explanation as he slipped into bed beside me. He put his hand gently on my stomach again and fell asleep.

I was confined to my bed for the next month and a half. This time it was my own choice. I was so sick that I felt like I needed to stay near my bathroom at all times. The doctor came to check on me twice before my three month appointment, but said that there was nothing wrong and that it was just an effect of the pregnancy. Antonio and his family were worried about me because I began to lose weight, rather than to gain it and I became increasingly weak.

One morning at the beginning of my second trimester I woke up feeling extremely hungry. I called down to the maid and she immediately brought up breakfast. I quickly ate everything on my plate and when nothing happened, I called Elena to let her know that food had finally stayed down. After hanging up with her, I asked the maid to bring me more immediately. She smiled at me and told me that she could see the color returning to my face.

After eating a third full plate, I took a shower and got dressed. I felt excitement grow as I left my room. I glanced down the hallway and quickly walked down the stairs to explore my house, something that I hadn't yet had the opportunity to do. I knew that Antonio was at a meeting so I didn't bother to call him to tell him that I was feeling better. I knew that he would be home around lunchtime. He could see for himself.

I was so happy to finally leave our room that I went into our kitchen to say hello to the maids. They didn't seem happy to see me in their space, so I quickly left the room. I stopped in our spacious living room and noticed that a huge portrait of Antonio and me hung on the wall. I didn't remember seeing it before and was a little upset that Antonio never brought it upstairs to show me the picture. I sat down directly in front of it and sat staring at it for a while I snacked on a banana I had grabbed while passing through the kitchen. One of the maids came in and brought me lunch without saying a word as she glanced at me nervously. I shrugged off her behavior and ate my food as I began to wonder where Antonio was. Had he been coming home for lunch after we found out about my pregnancy? I honestly didn't know. I had spent the majority of my time in bed, sleeping.

I ate alone and when I was finished the maid came and took my plate and asked if I would like anything else. I shook my head as I wiped my hands on a napkin.

I walked across the room to a table with a landline and called Antonio's cell phone but he didn't answer. I gazed around the room for a while longer, before getting bored. Elena had been busy when I called and said she would call back but hadn't yet. I wondered if I should call her back or wait. I couldn't believe that after being cooped up in my room for so long, it was possible for me to become bored. I sighed and stood up, deciding that I would explore the other rooms in the house.

At the bottom of the stairs, I found Antonio's study. I went to sit down on a brown leather chair behind his desk and looked at numerous pictures of him and other family members. I noticed that one picture frame was face down on a small table at the corner of the room and went over to pick it up. It was a picture of me. I remembered that Elena had taken that picture of me the day of her daughter's party. I picked it up so that my face was facing him whenever he sat at his desk and wondered if one of the maids had turned it over, or if it had simply fallen down. I bit down on my bottom lip as I looked around the room.

I stood up and walked across the room to a bookshelf, noticing that there were a few books written by Jane Austen. I remembered reading several of them with my mother as a child. I picked up one and sat down on a sofa that was in the room and began to read.

After an hour, I tried to call Antonio again, but still there was no answer and I began to get worried. I looked out the window, trying to find something unusual about the day and after a minute had passed I sat back down on the sofa, leaning back and without warning, fell asleep.

"Hey, what are you doing in here?" I heard Antonio ask as I slowly opened my eyes. "Are you feeling better?"

I nodded, glancing over at a clock on the wall, only to see that it was already four thirty.

"I'm sorry I'm so late." He said as he walked across the room and kissed me. "The meeting took longer than expected. What did you do today?"

I saw him glance at the table with my picture as he sat down at his desk. He nervously fiddled with a pen as he waited for my response.

"Nothing," I replied. "I missed you."

Antonio quickly waked across the room, hugged me and gave me a long kiss.

"Let's go upstairs," he suggested.

I smiled as he led me upstairs. Instead of taking me to our room as I hoped, he took me to the room across the hall. He motioned for me to follow him in.

"I figured this could be the baby's room."

I was disappointed as he began rattling off plans.

"What's wrong? We could knock down a wall if it's too small and we'll need to paint it, but I figured we won't do that until we know if it's a boy or a girl."

I shook my head as my eyes filled with tears.

"Oh Tony, that's not it," I replied. "I want you to make love to me. I feel like you think I'm hideous or something. You never touch me anymore."

Antonio sighed and shrugged at me as I stood before him, putting my hand to my face to hold back tears.

"Would that make you happy?" He asked playfully.

I nodded and smiled as I looked up at him.

"Okay." He replied. "I know have been neglecting my beautiful wife, so let's do this."

I grinned and we walked hand in hand across the hall to our room. I stripped off my clothes sexily in front of him as he smiled and took off his tie. I was down to my bra and panties when his cell phone rang. I felt my heart drop as he looked down at it before glancing back at me. I shook my head and tried to pull him to the bed.

28

"I have to get this." Antonio said apologetically. "Just get ready for me and I'll be off in a minute."

He answered the phone and I walked across the room, climbing into bed and removing my last articles of clothing as he stepped out of the room to have his conversation. A second later he came back in.

"I'm sorry baby, but I have to go." He said.

Tears welled in my eyes and I nodded and turned away. He sat down next to me and rubbed one of my shoulders and leaned over to kiss the other. I felt humiliated as I sat down on the bed, naked.

"I'm sorry, but now with the baby coming, I need all the business I can get. I promise I'll make it up to you when I get home."

I nodded without turning to him. He hugged me, put some cologne on and then left the room.

I slowly put my clothes back on and walked over to the window in our old room to watch him leave. I waved as if he could see me and then went to lie down on our old bed. For a few minutes, I just lay there and enjoyed the breeze. The sheer white curtains blew in the wind. I could feel my eyelids growing heavier and fell into a deep sleep. I didn't wake up again until the middle of the night. I was startled to still be in our old room and wondered why he hadn't woken me when he came home.

My stomach began to growl with hunger and I called out quietly for Antonio in the dark. When I didn't hear a response, I silently walked over to the window and saw that his car was there, along with Gilbert's. I walked across the hall to our room but he wasn't there. I put on my robe and left the room, going to the front stairway to look for him when I heard his voice downstairs. I knew immediately that he was in the study talking with Gilbert as both their jackets were hung on the coat rack.

I crept down the back stairway and snuck into the kitchen to make us both a snack, being very careful to be quiet because I didn't want Charles to wake up and offer to do it for me... or to see me in my robe, for that matter. I found a tray and loaded it with all kinds of goodies. Then I filled up two glasses with juice and carried everything on the trays down the hall toward the study. I smiled when I saw Gilbert sleeping in a chair nearby. I opened the door to the study by pushing it with my butt, not realizing that I had just heard Antonio talking with someone a few moments before and unaware that someone could be with him, besides Gilbert.

I turned as I walked in and, to my horror, Antonio was standing with his eyes closed and his pants down to his knees as he leaned against the desk. He was getting a blow-job from a red haired woman! His hand sat on top of my picture, which he had laid down upon the desk. I gasped and dropped the tray. They both turned around and I backed up only to realize that I had lost feeling in my legs and fell backwards onto my buttocks.

"Ow!" I cried out in pain as multiple pains shot through me.

Gilbert woke up and quickly jumped up to see what was going on. Antonio, who was still zipping up his pants, came out to help me and immediately started yelling at Gilbert.

"You were supposed to give me a warning, man!" Antonio shouted at him. "Unbelievable! Do I pay you to sleep?" Antonio said as he looked from side to side, not knowing what to do or to say to me as I sat with my face, covered in tears, in my hands.

Gilbert didn't say anything and I could hear Charles coming out of his room. Antonio leaned down and tried to hold me, but I backed away from him quickly and fell to my side.

My tears were uncontrollable, but I tried to sit up and yell at Antonio. "How could you?" I managed to get out of my throat.

Charles came running toward us with his robe on, seeing the redhead and exchanging looks with Antonio. Antonio backed away from me, putting his hand over his forehead and not knowing what to say. The redhead seemed to be gathering her things from the room and stopped to put my picture back upright on his desk.

"What happened?" She asked Antonio, but he said nothing as he handed the redhead her coat and told Gilbert to take her home.

"Don't move," she said to me, "you need a doctor."

"Ow!" I cried out in pain and tried to sit up again, determined not to listen to her.

"Antonio how could you?" I yelled with all the force that I could muster. "We're married."

As I yelled, I grasped my stomach in pain and felt a heavy rush between my legs. Antonio turned very pale as he stared down at me. I sobbed hard into my hands and looked around at everyone who had suddenly become quiet.

"What?" I asked them.

"You... you're bleeding." Antonio said to me.

I looked down and saw that the middle of my robe was covered in blood. "No." I shook my head and softly said. "No."

31

I tried to stand up but could feel myself falling to the side. I felt my face hit the floor hard and can remember pain rushing through my body. I fainted.

When I woke up again I was in a hospital room with. His eyes were wet from crying and he held my hand tightly. As soon as everything came into focus and I remembered what had happened, I quickly pulled my hand away. He immediately began to apologize.

"My baby," I said weakly, not listening to him as he talked.

I grabbed his hand again and pulled it toward me.

"The baby is ok?" I asked.

He shook his head as he stared apologetically at me.

"No." I said and began to cry as I snatched my hand back from him.

He tried to console me, putting his arms around me as he tried to hug and kiss me, but I pushed him away over and over again until he stopped. I sobbed to myself with him standing over me. When I finally pulled myself together I looked him right in the eye, my eyes full of rage.

"I want a divorce." I said, gritting my teeth as I spoke to him.

He shook his head.

"Not going to happen." He replied, this time his voice filled with anger. "There will be more chances for children."

"No." I said just as angrily. "That's not it. Do you think that I don't remember what happened, Tony? I saw you. How could you?" I asked him.

"I said that I was sorry." He said briskly.

"Is that it? Do you think that's going to make it better Tony?" I asked.

I sat still for a moment before shaking my head. "I want a divorce." I said again.

"No." He said, his voice beginning to fill with rage. "That will never happen. I would kill you before I allowed that. Don't test me, Lily."

He walked across the room, scaring me as his nostrils flared. He picked up a table and threw it across the room. I jumped, but did not let it scare me enough to remain quiet.

"In our religion there is no such thing as divorce." He said.

"Bullshit!" I screamed, my own words surprising me as they came out. "You were unfaithful to me. I hate you Tony."

"I was not." He screamed back. "I never had sex with that woman."

"Oh, so you just had your dick in her mouth?" I screamed back at him, my chest filling with pain.

"That's not the same!"

"Oh my God..." I said quietly before going into a screaming fit. "Oh my God, Antonio. Do you really expect me to believe that?"

I picked up a phonebook from the table beside me and threw it at him. "How could I ever be with you again?" I screamed at him angrily.

"Think about it." He replied coldly. "I am the only one that cares about you."

I sat silently as my heart seemed to drop into my stomach.

"What are you going to do if you leave me?" He asked without waiting for an answer. "You have nothing!"

I sat quietly for a moment and glanced out the window across the room. His words felt like a knife as they seemed to stick the inside of my chest. I felt as if I couldn't breathe. "You, care about me?" I sputtered in a low voice and looked over at him.

He nodded as he walked back toward the bed.

"Come on now, Antonio." I said, my voice raising as I spoke. I looked down at my hands and then up at him. "You chose a really bad way to show it!" I yelled across the room at him, as a nurse walked into the room.

"Can you please keep it down in here?" She said briskly. "This is the recovery unit."

She suddenly realized who Antonio was and apologized and walked out of the room.

"Call Elena." I ordered him.

"No." He replied quickly. "Not until you calm down, besides she's probably sleeping at this time." He said as he glanced down at his watch.

"Well get over it because I'm not calming down." I snarled at him. "I need her, not you."

"Lily, calm down." He said sternly.

"No." I replied. "You're not my father."

"Oh and do you think that if I was your father, your life would be so much better?" He asked. "I'm your husband and I said to calm down."

"You're not much of a husband." I spat out at him, hardly getting the words out of my mouth.

He stood over me and slapped me hard across the face. He backed away and immediately apologized.

"Get out of here." I screamed, my face stinging in pain.

I saw the nurse walk by and instead of coming in to help, she shut the door.

I began sobbing. Who was I kidding? This was my life and this was how it would be. I cried so hard that I started choking and sat up. When I did, he held me. I tried to pull away from him, but there was no use. I collapsed in his arms, choking on my tears as he began to rub my back. I could feel him crying with me and this only made anger shoot through my body. He stroked my hair and whispered into my ear.

"I'm sorry." He said again and again.

I didn't respond to him as he spoke. I'm sorry doesn't cut it, I thought to myself. How could he have put me in this position? How could I have put myself in this position? In all honesty, I hardly knew him before we got married. I wondered what my mother thought of me as she looked down from the heavens. My life was such a failure. I felt hurt and betrayed. On top of everything else, I was so sad for losing my baby and confused because I still loved this horrible man with all of my heart. I pulled away and gazed up at him with sad eyes.

"I need some time apart." I said softly, holding my hand out and touching his chin. "I think I'll ask Elena if I can stay with her for a while."

"No," Antonio replied. "How would that look?"

"Is that all you care about?" I asked. "It will look even worse if word gets out that I want a divorce." I sighed as I looked around the room. "You can tell everyone that I am staying with her until I recover," I said softly. "And no one has to know why I'm really there."

He shook his head again in disbelief but thought about it for a while as he sat across from me. Finally he nodded and agreed to go along with it. He apologized again and quickly left the hospital room without looking back at me.

I didn't need to call Elena. She showed up to come and get me about an hour later. Elena was sad for the loss of the baby but she said she was thrilled at the thought of me moving in for a time. I knew that she felt lonely with Miguel, just as I did with Antonio. We lived a different type of life. It was a life that couldn't be claimed as our own. We left the hospital in silence that morning.

Chapter Two

I stayed with Elena for close to six months. For the first couple of weeks that I was there, I would not come out of my room. I knew Antonio was there every day because I could hear him talking to Elena and her husband just outside of my doorway. He never tried to come into the room. I told Elena that I didn't want to see him and she relayed the message to him. For once, Miguel agreed with Elena and told Antonio that it was better that he didn't come in to see me.

I would move to different corners of the room to sit and read, but with the attached bathroom, there was no reason for me to even walk out into the hallway.

Elena made it a point to bring my meals in to me herself and she would sit and talk with me. I was very short with her and although she was trying to help me, I wouldn't let her. I was in my own world and I didn't want her or anyone else to be a part of it. After a while I saw that I was causing Elena pain and tried to start answering her in complete sentences and even to ask her questions about her day. It felt unreal to me, but I knew that I had to pretend. I felt as if everyone was looking at me like I was a fool, including Elena.

How could I have not known? I felt like it was my fault that everything happened. I finally decided to discuss my thoughts on this with Elena and she sighed. She shook her head and took me in her arms, telling me that I was wrong. She talked with me for hours, telling me about the failed relationships of her friends and cousins. Some of the couples chose to stay together and some split up. None of the couples she talked about were married though. I asked her about that and she told me that to her family, once you are married, you have to learn how to work your problems out.

Miguel came to the room and said they had to take the kids to his parents' house for a visit. As soon as I knew they were gone, I decided to leave the room and snuck out very quietly. I walked out to the side gate of the house, nodding at one of the guards at the gate. I pushed the button to open it myself and walked through. He looked puzzled and I quickly regretted leaving as I saw him reach for his phone. I continued walking down the street quickly, determined to get as far away from the house as possible.

It was a beautiful day and I could feel the sun heating up my cold body. I could hear birds chirping from trees overhead and I couldn't help but notice that the outside world looked happy and full of life. I continued to walk quickly, breaking into a jog as I passed the gas station. Soon I reached the town square and some vendors began coming at me trying to sell me things, while others stared at me with puzzled expressions. I kept walking. I had no money to buy anything even if I wanted to.

As I turned a corner, I saw the church in the distance and decided I would go there and pray for myself and my family. When I was about a block away from the church I saw a car pass and cringed. It slammed on its breaks and reversed to me. I couldn't help stopping in my tracks and staring at the car. I knew that it was Antonio, even before he rolled down the window. I glanced away the second our eyes met. He didn't say anything for a minute, he just stared at me.

"Lily, get in the car." He finally said angrily.

"No." I replied.

"We had an agreement." He said. "Where are you going?"

I sighed and glanced to the side. It was apparent that he was not going to leave me alone.

"To church." I replied fearfully.

The look on his face made me feel scared that he would jump out of the car and pull me in. I wouldn't put anything past him at this point.

"To see who?" He asked.

I shot him a disgusted look and his expression softened into a smile.

"I'll go with you." He said, when I didn't return his smile.

I didn't say anything. I just turned and started walking. He followed slowly behind me in his car. When we arrived at the church I paused as he parked and jumped out, rushing to my side to follow me in. He grabbed my hand when we got inside and I quickly pulled it away. I went to a pew in the middle of the church and he followed me and sat down before I did. Instead of sitting, I turned to him.

"I need to do this on my own." I muttered.

I walked away and moved three aisles up. He shot me an angry glare as I returned his expression, before turning away. I could feel his stern gaze burning the back of my neck.

I knelt down on the bench and glanced up at the mural of Jesus on the cross. I crossed my hand to my forehead, chest and both sides of my face and began to pray. I prayed first for my mother and then for the child that I had lost. I was trying to avoid praying for myself but soon I found myself asking Christ to save my marriage. I felt foolish for asking. I wasn't even sure if I still loved Antonio, moments later I asked God to help me determine which way to go with our marriage as well. I silently stood up, forgetting that Antonio was behind me.

As I turned to leave, Antonio was immediately at my side. I opened my mouth to tell him to get away from me, but before the words came out I saw the priest standing at the door watching us. I sighed and allowed him to grab onto my arm. As we walked by the priest I forced a smile.

"Good morning Father." Antonio said as we continued to walk past him.

The priest walked behind us quietly, I assumed to see us out of the church.

"Perdóname." The priest said to us.

The priest shook his head and smiled, probably remembering that I did not speak Spanish and then proceeding to speak to us in English as best as he could.

"I'm sorry for your loss." He said slowly.

Antonio nodded at him and glanced at me.

"Sometimes the timing isn't right and God gives us a little more time to prepare ourselves for better things to come." The priest said, nodding, and then pressed his lips together.

I forced a smile. Instead of being filled with sadness at his comment, I was filled with curiosity. I wondered how the priest had found out about the baby. Antonio put his arm around my waist and led me out.

"The priest is informed of all births and deaths in this town." Antonio said to me, as if to read my thoughts.

I broke free from his grip and stood still at the side of the church as he started to walk to his car. He stopped and turned to me. "Are you going back to Elena's house?" He asked biting down on his lip.

I nodded and turned away.

"Can I give you a ride back?" He asked.

In my head I thought over telling him that I'd sooner die, but I looked back at the church and decided that this wasn't the right time or place to do that. I proceeded to quickly get into the car without responding to him. Antonio looked at me uncomfortably, as though he wanted to say something. He stared at me for at least a minute without speaking. Finally he started the car. Antonio smiled lightly and began to drive towards Elena's house.

"Can I buy you dinner?" He asked.

"No, thank you." I replied.

Silence filled the car as he continued to drive as slowly out of the town. There were only a few cars on our route and the drivers drove past us, looking back at Antonio with a dirty look. One driver opened his mouth as if about to say something, but Antonio rolled down his window and the driver realized who Antonio was and sped off. Antonio smirked at himself in the mirror and continued to drive slowly. Antonio turned on the radio, only to quickly turn it off seconds later, glancing over at me as he did. He pulled to the side of the road and turned off the car as I braced myself for whatever he had to say and debated on getting out and walking the rest of the way back to Elena's house.

"Please don't make me take you back there, Lily." He said to me.

His words took me off guard as I stared into his dark brown eyes. His lip began to tremble.

"I love you so much." He said with a sincere expression. "I am so sorry."

I glanced over at him. Even though he looked sincere, I couldn't forgive him. It hurt me not to reach over and hold him, but I couldn't forget about what he had done. I had the image of him with his pants down forever ingrained into my mind. I put my hand to my forehead and watched as a tear fell from his face. I felt an overwhelming sadness come over me as I watched him. I reached over and touched his shoulder to get his attention.

"I can't, Tony." I said softly to him. "I just can't."

"Please." He begged me again. "Do you know everyone is telling me that I shouldn't give you the choice, that I should just take you home and be done with it?"

Antonio sighed and looked to the side. I could feel my hands begin to sweat. I looked down at them and then wiped them on my legs nervously.

"I can't do that Lily." He said. "I want you to be happy. I want you to want to come home."

He glanced at me, but I said nothing. I turned my head to look out the window.

"I know that I was wrong." He blurted out. "I know that you were there for me and I was wrong. I don't know what I was thinking."

He sat silently waiting for a response. A car drove slowly by us. The passenger looked over at us to see if everything was okay. Antonio nodded his head at him and the car drove on.

"I love you." He said, turning back to me. "I love you so much, Lily. Please can we at least work on it? I'm not letting you divorce me, so we might as well work on it."

I sighed. It pained me to see him sad. I loved him so much. The more that I listened to him spilling his thoughts out to me, the more I realized how much I loved him and how much I missed him.

"Okay, we can work on it." I said without looking at him.

He immediately took me in his arms and held me tightly.

"You'll see, Lily." He said happily. "When you come back home, I will make everything up to you."

I pulled away.

"I don't know if I can ever go back there." I said. "I have so many bad memories."

"What if I buy us a different house, will you come back then?" He asked.

I shrugged my shoulders and he kissed my forehead. He gazed into my eyes, trying to find an answer that I wasn't ready to give him. I looked away. He sighed and started up the car. We drove back to Elena's house in silence. As soon as we arrived, I saw Elena and Miguel's heads disappear from a downstairs window. It seemed that there were other people waiting for us as well. When we entered the house, I noticed several glasses set on tables in the now empty living room.

Antonio paused as we walked into the room and sat down in the sofa, motioning for me to sit down beside him. I

43

reluctantly sat down next to him, waiting for him to say something. He glanced around the room, as if he were looking for a clue as to how to get started. Catalina cleared her throat and entered the room. She set down a plate of appetizers on the table and began picking up the glasses from the tables around us. She glanced back at us as she turned to go in the kitchen.

"Sometimes, it's difficult to forgive others, but it's pertinent to our existence." She said firmly and left the room.

I knew her words were directed at me and I smiled nervously at her as she left the room. Antonio grabbed my hand in his and held it still. I allowed him to hold it without looking up at him. His hand was warm and it felt good as he surrounded my fingers with his grasp. We sat for what felt like hours in that same position. Finally I turned to him and looked him into his eyes.

"I'm tired." I said as I stood up. "I think I'm going to go to bed."

I quickly walked up the stairs without looking back. As I closed the door to my room, I heard Elena and Miguel and a few other voices begin to question him about what had happened. I lay down silently in my bed without falling asleep. I thought about everything that we had gone through and wondered if I would be able to find forgiveness in my heart.

The next week flew by quickly. Antonio was at Elena's house every day trying to woo me with flowers and candy. I would go on walks with him and eat dinner with him. Eventually it made less and less sense to me to continue to live separately from him. No sooner then I began thinking about going back on my own did he tell me that he would be going to the United States for three months and that I could have the house to myself if I came home. I agreed to move back in with him, knowing that I had overstayed my welcome with Elena and Miguel. I knew that Miguel didn't approve of Antonio pleading with me to come home the last couple weeks. I had overheard him say some really bad things about the way Antonio was allowing me to act.

As we drove home that night, Antonio and I sat in silence. I told myself that I would try my best to reestablish our relationship. I glanced over at him as we drove. He focused on the road and I wondered if the same thoughts were going through his mind. His phone rang countless times. Different people called him in regard to his trip. He kept it short with them and tried his best to focus on me.

When we arrived at home, the usual maids were not there to greet us, instead I saw new faces. Antonio ran through a list of names and what they did, but I paid little attention. I grabbed onto his arm as he turned to lead me to the dining room. There was no way that I would remember everyone's name. I would talk with them more after Antonio left.

"Where's Charles and the others." I asked him quietly.

Antonio bit down on his lip and took a good amount of time to think over his reply.

"Oh, his mother was ill and he and his sisters went to be with her." He said. "Is dinner ready?" He called out to a stout woman.

She nodded and ushered us into the dining room. Antonio seemed nervous as he glanced over at me.

"We're going to need a bottle of wine for our homecoming celebration." He said to her.

She nodded again and left the room. I grabbed his arm quickly.

"I don't want to drink." I said.

"Come on baby." He replied. "One won't hurt. It'll just loosen us up a bit so we can talk. I don't know about you, but I'm feeling nervous."

"Just one." I replied.

He fought a wicked smile with no success. He was right, I told myself. I felt like I needed a drink. I was so tense that I felt like I needed it to help me loosen me up and to get comfortable in our home. As we ate dinner, I did only have one glass of wine. The problem was that every time I took a sip the stout woman would walk by and refill my glass. By the time I was done eating. I couldn't stand up straight. Antonio came around to my side of the table and smiled at me. He helped me up to our room and laid me across the bed as he began to strip my clothes off.

"No." I said softly. "What are you doing? I'm not ready for this yet."

I tried to push him off of me, but he began to kiss every inch of my body. He moved his head between my legs and began flicking his tongue about. Within seconds, I was burning with desire and there was no use trying to fight it. I let him continue and just lay back on the bed quietly. He lay down on top of me and slipped his manhood into me slowly. I sighed in pain and put my hand to his chest to push him away. It had been some time and my insides seemed to tighten up.

"Come on baby." He said to me as he continued, softly whispering into my ear. "I'm going to be gone for three months. Leave me with something good to remember."

He paused for a moment until I wrapped my arm around his neck and pulled him toward me, giving him the sign to continue. I shuddered as he moaned in pleasure, penetrating my body deeper and deeper. I felt tears fall from my face as I looked to the side to avoid looking at him as he moved above me. I loved how it felt. I wanted to trust him but I just didn't. Suddenly there was an eruption of warmth inside me and he stopped. He lay still without moving for a long while. He moved to the side of me and I fell asleep in his arms.

The next morning he shook me gently, calling my name softly until I opened one eye. He was already dressed and had his bag packed, ready to leave. I felt embarrassed as I realized that I lay naked on top of the sheets.

"I'll call you every day." He said.

I wanted to ask him to stay, but I didn't. I sat up in bed and watched him, as he called Marcus to let him know that he was ready and then called the hotel to make sure of the time that he would be able to check in. The sun had just begun to rise. Daylight gleamed into our room. I didn't say a word until he was finished with what he was doing and came over to give me one final kiss. He grabbed my hand as he pulled away.

"Mi amor." He said. "I promise you that I will never stray again."

I quickly looked away. I couldn't bear being lied to.

"I'm going to prove it to you." He said. "You'll see".

He turned to leave and I ran over to him and kissed him again, passionately. He lifted me up in his arms and threw me down on the bed. I clung to his shirt collar as he undid his pants and quickly slipped inside me. I wrapped my legs around him tightly as he entered my body again and again furiously. Marcus knocked on the door a minute later.

"Just a minute." Antonio called and finished off while I began to laugh.

Antonio dressed quickly when he was done and picked up the suitcase.

"I love you," he turned to me and said.

I nodded but didn't say anything as I put on my robe. I decided to wait until he proved himself to me before I told him anything like that again. I got up to hug him and kissed him on the cheek.

He stared at me for a moment and then opened the door.

"Good morning." Marcus said.

"Good morning," I replied as he leaned over to kiss my cheek.

"It's good to see you back at home." Marcus said. "Tony missed you very much while you were away and so did the rest of us."

"Are you going to the United States with Antonio?" I asked.

I didn't want to say that I had missed him. Antonio didn't need to know that. Marcus glanced at Antonio. Something seemed very strange to me about their expressions.

"Yes we are." Marcus replied to me. "I promise to bring him back in one piece."

I thought that his reply was a little odd, but I didn't bring it up. Instead we said our goodbyes and they were gone.

Roberta came over about an hour later and we relaxed in the pool for the remainder of the day. I had dinner that night alone. The cook was very short with me. I guessed that I couldn't befriend her, or any of the other staff for that matter. She left a small package with my dinner when she brought it to me. I studied the box curiously until I was finished eating. The food she made had no seasoning and tasted horrible. When I swallowed my last bite of food, I opened the package. Inside of the package was a cell phone, with a note. I had never owned a cellphone in my life. The note read:

"Hi mi Amor. Call me when you open this."

I paused for a minute and then dialed his number. Antonio answered on the first ring and I laughed.

"I've been waiting for your call." He said. "Press the button with my face on it."

I did as he instructed and suddenly I could see him. I smiled.

"I just finished eating." I said.

"Ah yes." He asked. "How was it?"

"Not good." I replied quietly, looking around the room to make sure the cook hadn't heard me.

"Can I at least have Catalina since I came back home?" I asked him, laughing.

"We'll see." He replied. "I'll mention it to Elena and if I find out that she's available, even if it's just for a day. I'll get her."

"Good. No one around here has a friendly bone in their body. I feel so uncomfortable." I replied. "I thought the other maids were mean. These ladies are ten times worse. They don't even smile."

"Don't feel that way." He replied. "It's your home, not theirs."

I smiled and glanced around the room. It still didn't feel like my home. It never had.

"Did you take a shower yet?" He asked.

"No not yet." I replied. "I was in the pool all day with Roberta."

"Oh, Roberta came over?" He asked. "I'll have to mention something to Marcus."

"Why?" I asked. "Wasn't she supposed to?"

"No, it's not that." He replied. "It was just nice of her. I'll have to thank him."

"She's a nice person." I replied.

"Yes she is." Antonio said.

"Baby. Why don't you take a bath today?" He asked. "Take it with me on the phone. I'll pretend I'm there."

"What?" I asked and laughed out loud and looked at his face peering at me through the phone.

"Um. Okay." I said slowly.

I began to walk up the stairs.

"Hey Tony," I asked as I attempted to figure out where he was from the background of his picture.

"Yes." He replied.

"What part of the United States are you in anyway?" I asked.

Antonio remained silent for a moment. He glanced behind him at the wall.

"Sweetie. I can't lie to you." He said. "I'm not in the United States, I'm in Venezuela."

"What?" I asked. "You're not far then."

"Why do you need to stay there for so long?" I asked. "Can't you come home sooner?"

"I'll try to, baby." He said. "Right now it's hard. We're taking a class, Marcus and me and a few other guys."

"Oh." I replied quietly. "Why'd you lie to me? Why didn't you tell me that's where you were going to be?"

"Venezuela is a dangerous place sweetie." He said. "I didn't want you to be worried."

"Colombia is pretty dangerous too." I said. "Roberta and I watched the afternoon news before we went to the pool..."

Antonio immediately cut me off by breathing heavily into the phone.

"Don't watch the news baby, okay?" He asked. "The news is full of horrible stories. Those news people will say anything to sell a story. Don't watch it and don't read it, okay? Promise me that."

I paused for a moment.

"Okay, Tony." I said, knowing it was true. "I promise."

The news here was a lot worse then I remembered it in America. Many times the news showed actual dead bodies and told stories of horrible tragedies. I went upstairs and ran the bath water while talking to Antonio.

"Colombia has gotten a lot safer over the years." He said. "Still, I worry about you so much."

I propped the phone up on the toilet and stripped off my clothes seductively in front of the phone. I could see him bite down on his lip. I picked up the phone, laughing and set it on the sink, positioning it to where we could see each other from my seat in the bathtub. I proceeded to get in and we talked for about four hours until I almost fell asleep from the sound of his voice.

"Baby, wake up." I heard him say. "Wake up."

I opened my eyes slowly.

"What... Oh, sorry Tony, I was falling asleep." I said.

"I know you were." He replied, laughing. "Now get out of the bath and go get dressed. Keep the phone with you tomorrow. Make sure you charge it up. I'll call you tomorrow when our classes are done."

"Okay Tony." I said. "I miss you."

"I love you." He said.

I smiled at him through the phone, still not believing that I could see him, before hanging up. I dried myself off and put on my pajamas before going to sleep in our comfortable bed.

He called every day that he was gone and after about three weeks I didn't hesitate in telling him that I loved him. I felt very close to him even though he was gone. I knew he had changed. I could hear it in the tone of his voice. I hoped that he would be able to come back sooner than anticipated. Three months was a long time to be away from each other.

Chapter Three

The next three months went by quickly. Antonio's family members came to spend the day with me just about every day. Everyone took turns coming over, everyone except for Blanca. At first I felt offended that she didn't come over. I felt like we had become fairly close for a while, but when I needed her most, she abandoned me. I made excuses for her, in order to make myself feel better, and in her defense she did call me regularly and apologized for not coming to visit. She often said that she was ill or that Elena needed her help with something at her house. There were some points that I wondered if she was upset with me, but for the most part, I was glad that she didn't come to the house.

Antonio had only been gone a month and a half when I figured out that I was pregnant. I decided not tell Antonio about my pregnancy over the phone. It wouldn't be long before he was back and I wanted to see his reaction when I told him. The problem was that I wouldn't be able to see the doctor without him. It simply wasn't allowed in our small and outdated town. I debated on going to the city to see a doctor on my own, but that would be a long and dangerous trip to take on my own.

I begged Antonio every night to come home sooner, not disclosing to him my reason in doing so. I made sure that when we spoke using video on the phone, I didn't show him anything below the neck. He noticed after a while when he asked me to strip for him and I declined his requests, telling him that this was my way of getting him home sooner. When he told me that he was trying, I told him to try harder.

I couldn't believe that I was pregnant. We had only slept together those two times since I came home. I was dying to tell someone and ordinarily my next pick would have been Elena, but she was on vacation for the summer and was unreachable. She would be coming home around the time Antonio was so, I figured that I would wait to tell her after I told him.

By the time Antonio had been gone for three months, I was really starting to show. I was worried that Antonio suspected something, as we talked over the phone. Most of the weight that I had put on was in my upper body including my face, which had even expanded at least an inch. My nose even stretched out. I finally decided to tell Roberta but made her promise not to tell her husband. She helped me to disguise my pregnancy so that no one else in the family would catch on. She did express her concerns with not seeing a doctor yet, but I assured her that Antonio would be home soon and everything would be fine.

I'm sure the housekeepers were beginning to suspect something but if they were, they didn't say anything. Our cook had grown colder with me, so rather than to bother her with my requests, I went into the kitchen to prepare my own food. Her cooking wasn't that great anyhow. The good thing about my pregnancy was that I didn't have morning sickness, but the downside was that I was always hungry and I ate like a pig. I snuck downstairs after getting off the phone with Antonio every night to get more food.

I looked in the mirror every night before going to sleep and was surprised at how big my stomach was for being three months pregnant. In addition during this time where I should have been completely happy, the visions of my last pregnancy lurked in my mind. I tried to push the thoughts out of my mind and I felt worried about how our relationship would fit back together upon his return. Antonio called to say his return date had been postponed a few weeks. He was now scheduled to come home on his birthday, three weeks later than I had been expecting him.

I was sad about the delay but decided to plan a surprise party for Antonio at which I would reveal my pregnancy. Roberta got me in touch with her cousin, Freddie who was a party planner and she suggested that he plan the party. I wanted to plan the party myself but after sitting down to talk with the two of them, I realized how much work it would be. I didn't know what types of stores were in the area or where I would be able to buy things from. On top of that, Roberta said that since Antonio was her Godson she would pay for it. I also couldn't ask Antonio for money to pay for his own surprise party.

Freddie came over a few times to go over all the arrangements and I became more and more excited about how everything was moving along. Freddie was able to make Roberta's money go a long way because of his connections in the industry. On his last visit, a week before the party, Blanca popped in on us unexpectedly. We were sitting out in the garden going over the entertainment and she shot right up to us, coming out of nowhere.

"What's going on?" She asked loudly, as her eyes scanned the room.

"Oh. Hi Blanca." I replied. "This is Roberta's cousin Freddie. He's putting together Antonio's surprise birthday party."

"What party?" Blanca asked. "I didn't hear anything about a party."

A shiver went through my body. How was I going to explain to her that I hadn't sent out invitations? We never sent out invitations when we had barbeques, I had forgotten that they were a requirement.

"Oh, you know Antonio is coming home next week on his birthday." I exclaimed, glancing over at Freddie. "I'm planning to throw him a surprise party when he arrives. I was planning to call everyone tomorrow. I figured it was still a week away."

Blanca gritted her teeth together and stared at Freddie. He was a pretty attractive guy, but he had nothing on Antonio.

"Humph." She snorted. "Surprise?"

She glared at Freddie and me intensely. Just then my cell phone rang and I leaned over to pick it up.

"Hello. Oh, hi Tony." I said, holding my belly as I sat back up.

"I'd better go." Freddie said quietly.

I nodded and stood up. Freddie gathered up his paperwork and exited from the side door of the house. Blanca was staring at me hard.

"Is that my son? Let me talk to him." She ordered, taking the phone from me without waiting for an answer.

I looked down as she walked off with the phone talking quickly in Spanish. I noticed that my shirt had tucked itself under my stomach. I quickly pulled it out and hoped that Blanca did not notice my very pregnant stomach. She watched me as she spoke and walked further away from me. Finally she handed me the phone.

"I'm leaving." She said and quickly stormed off.

I put the phone back up to my ear.

"Lily. Lily?" Antonio screamed into the receiver.

"I'm here." I replied, feeling somewhat confused.

"What's going on?" He yelled into the phone. "Who's there?"

"Huh." I said sitting down in a nearby chair. "No one is here now. Your mom just stormed off like a mad woman."

"No one's there?" He asked loudly. "Who was there a moment ago when she arrived?"

I was silent for a minute. I couldn't tell him about the party. I knew he might know Roberta's cousin and what he did if I told him a name. I didn't say anything for a minute, knowing how bad everything was going to sound.

"A friend." I replied softly.

"Tell me about your friend." He replied loudly.

"I'll tell you about it when you come home Tony." I replied. "You have to trust me."

The call was lost. I tried calling him back several times but received his voice mail each time. I ate dinner and watched a couple of movies. It was very late, but I couldn't fall asleep. I decided to go for a swim in our Mediterranean style indoor pool. As I walked out of my room I glanced down the hallway, noting that the house staff was probably already sleeping because the house was quiet. I took my phone with me in case Antonio decided to call back. I slowly climbed into the water and swam across the pool when I heard voices shouting and doors slamming followed by footsteps. I got out of the pool and walked around the side of the room cautiously. I heard more voices and then I heard Antonio call my name.

"I'm in here." I called out, forgetting how upset he had sounded on the phone. "By the pool."

I walked quickly over to the door and threw my arms around him the second I saw him looking up at him for a kiss.

Instead of seeing his lips perched he glared around the room, his nostrils flaring as he spoke.

"You're swimming at this time?" He asked, pushing me away. "Who's here?"

"No one. I was stressed out, so I decided to go for a swim." I said smiling. "I'm so happy to see you."

He glared at me hard and then proceeded to search the room.

"Where is he?" He asked.

"What?" I asked. "Where is who?"

"The man that was here earlier." He snarled back at me.

"Oh do you mean Freddie?" I asked. He's gone.

"So a man was here?" He replied loudly. "In my house."

"Yes, but Tony what are you getting mad for?" I quickly replied. "You have to hear me out. He's just helping me with a few things."

I debated on telling him about the party and decided that I would have to just as Antonio's mother appeared in the doorway with a bag.

"You see Antonio." She said motioning at me. "I told you something was going on."

"You think I go to work to support you so that you can be with other men." Antonio screamed at me.

I grabbed his hand, but he snatched it back from me.

"Antonio I'm not with other men." I said, turning away from him.

"And today?" He screamed.

"Antonio, Freddie's gay." I said.

"He's gay?" Blanca said to herself, laughing.

"Antonio that man was not gay!" She said. "He ran out of here as soon as I got here."

I stared at her open mouthed for a minute. I suddenly realized how bad the incident must have looked.

"You have no right to doubt me." I said, turning to Blanca. "That was Roberta's cousin, you can ask her Tony."

I sighed and looked around the garden that the pool sat in. I could tell the maids were up. I could see their shadows from the windows of the rooms surrounding us as they eavesdropped on our conversation.

"I haven't even seen you in three months and you start this mess." I said angrily to her. "Stay out of our relationship!"

"That's right three months Antonio." Blanca said. "It seems longer."

She stared at my stomach hard.

"When was the last time you were with her intimately Antonio?" She asked.

"Three months ago." Antonio replied quietly as he stared at my stomach that revealed my pregnant stomach popping out from the elastic in my bathing suit.

"And before that?" Blanca asked.

"Not for some time." Antonio said.

"Let's see." Blanca asked. "Since the miscarriage? Sweetheart, does that belly look like it is only three months pregnant?"

Antonio didn't look at me as she questioned him.

"You've been around enough pregnant women to know that you don't show that much at only three months." Blanca spit out. "She looks like she is five or six months along. She's probably been seeing that man all along."

I was livid. My face was on fire and I held my hands at my side to restrain myself from choking her.

"Then she has men in and out of the house while you're away." She continued on. "What kind of a wife is she?"

My mouth dropped open as she spoke. My eyes filled with tears. I knew my stomach was big, but I didn't think that I looked like I was six months pregnant.

"Antonio you know me." I said, attempting to approach him. "I have never lied to you. This is your baby. I was going to tell you when you came home. That's why I've been begging you to hurry home."

I turned to Antonio's mother Blanca who gripped the suitcase toughly.

"How dare you." I exclaimed.

"Humph." Blanca said. "How dare I, the tramp asks?"

She held out the bag.

"Tramp?" I asked, loudly.

Antonio walked to her side and nodded for me to take the bag.

"Tony!" I exclaimed without moving. "I was locked in your sister's house five or six months ago. How could you suspect that this is not your baby?"

"I don't believe you Lily." Antonio said sternly. "We caught you with a man."

"What?" I asked, my bottom lip quivering.

"You heard me Lily." Antonio said. "I think it's best if you go before you create any more embarrassment for my family."

"Embarrassment?" I asked.

Antonio wasn't listening. Instead he was going through the bag and pulling out clothes that I instantly recognized. My lips began to quiver harder. I recognized the clothes as the ones that I had took with me when I left my father's house when we were married. He threw me my old house robe. It landed on the floor at my feet.

"Here, put this on." Antonio said. "I think this is all that you have here that will fit."

I stood aghast as I picked it up and put it on.

"What are you doing Tony?" I asked.

I tried to make eye contact with him but he looked away. I slowly put my hands into the robe, deciding that I would put it on and go up to our room to get away from his mother.

Blanca and my eyes met. Her gaze was cold and told me that something horrible was about to happen. A cool breeze hit my wet skin, the hairs on my arms begun to stand up as she stared at me. Two of the guards from the front gate entered the room. I wiped my tears and tried to smile at them to greet them. They didn't smile back and their eyes seemed to look right through me.

"What's going on Tony?" I asked, my voice cracking with each word.

Antonio walked away without looking at me and the guards now stood at each side of me. Blanca smiled at me.

"Time for you to go." She said, turning away.

"What?" I asked. "What's going on Tony? Tony, you have to believe me."

The guards put their hands around either side of my upper arm and began to lead me out of the house, stopping only to let me put my slippers on. I saw Antonio walking up the stairs to our room as I was walked into the hallway.

"Tony!" I called. "Tony, what are you doing? I never cheated on you... Why would I lie? Where are they taking me? What are you doing Tony? I love you Tony, you know that."

I continued to scream out to him from across the room like a crazy woman. Antonio paused on the stairs but didn't turn around. Soon I was outside, but the guards didn't stop walking. It was dark outside. The mosquitos started to bite my moist skin.

"Wait." I said to them. "I don't have my phone. Wait. What are you doing?"

I felt the cool ground and then the rocks beneath my feet, as they were only protected by my slippers. The guards took me all the way outside of the gate and then left me there.

"Wait." I exclaimed but they left my side and walked back inside the gate quickly, closing it behind them.

I stood there for a minute dumbfounded. Then I began pleading with them to let me back inside. After I received no response from either of the guards, I began to sob and leaned against the gate. I lowered myself to the ground and sat on the moist ground, trying to shield myself from the mosquitos.

"Great," I murmured. "It must have rained earlier, just my luck."

I sat on the ground for the entire night watching the guards without falling asleep. One of the younger guards looked at me with pity in his eyes. Every time our eyes met, he looked away. I closed my eyes and leaned my head against the gate a few hours later and drifted into a light sleep. I woke up not long after to the sound of chirping birds. The sun was not up yet but I knew morning had come. I managed to stand up though I had a horrible cramping sensation in my legs. Not far away, down the hill leading to our house the merchants were setting up their outdoor market as usual. I began to walk away from the gate in order to get the cramps out of my legs.

"What a sight I must be." I muttered to myself.

I wondered how often they saw a person in their house robe sleeping outside. My stomach began to rumble. I glanced down the hill at a few of the merchants that I knew would be selling food. I had no money to buy anything and wondered if they would give me a sample at least to tide me over. I decided that I would try to get back in the house one last time. The sky looked gray, though the sun was coming up now. I knew that it would probably rain later.

There I was completely alone again in the world that I thought I knew something about. I wondered back up the hill to our house, my stomach growling. I engaged a guard in conversation and almost thought I had him to the point where he would open the gate when I saw Gilbert driving Tony's SUV toward the end of the driveway and I ran to the side of the gate. Gilbert looked me in the eye and shook his head. The guard at the gate told me to get away, but I stood there as Gilbert pulled out. He drove slowly past me, the windows down since it was early. Horror struck my soul as I could see

Antonio there in the backseat with a blonde woman kissing her, stopping momentarily to glance over at me.

I gasped and stepped away from the gate holding my stomach. I saw the younger guard shake his head at me from the corner of the eye. I felt a pain race through my stomach and my heart began to pound loud enough that I could hear it pulsating in my eardrums. I felt like someone had just stabbed me as I staggered down the hill feeling overwhelmed and like my feet didn't want to carry me.

I walked over to one merchants table and asked him if I could please have a bottle of water and that I would pay him later. He shook his head at me and gave me a hand signal to indicate that I needed to give him money. He said something loudly which caused all of the other vendors to stop and notice me pathetically standing at his cart in my bathrobe. I turned to leave and as I walked by some people, they spit at my feet. I felt so disgusted that if I had any food in my stomach, I would have vomited.

I walked as far away from the crowd as possible. Then I sat down on the sidewalk and lowered my head. I sat completely still for what felt like an hour. Sweat began to drip from my neck from the heat of the sun. A woman came over to me with a bottle of water and a bag of chips, touching my back as I sat there to get my attention. I turned to her and thanked her as she quietly walked away.

It occurred to me that I had to do the unthinkable. I got up and began to walk to my father's house slowly while drinking my water and eating my chips. By the time I got there it was two in the afternoon and Madrigal had already gotten out of school. Upon turning into my old neighborhood, I noticed that she was sitting on her friend's porch eating an ice cream cone. I couldn't believe how much she had grown up in the last two years. She looked up and smiled broadly, waving at me and immediately looked excited as she came running over to me.

"Liliana, Liliana," she cried as she wrapped her arms around me. Her hand brushed against the fabric on my robe.

"What happened to your clothes?" She asked.

Before I could answer she looked up at me and smiled.

"You're going to have a baby? I'm going to be an Aunt?" She said all together with excitement.

I smiled back and nodded trying to keep a happy face for her.

"Antonio made me leave." I said quietly, trying not to stutter as I spoke.

Just then I heard my father call her into the house. He came out of the house and stared at me. His wife walked onto the porch as he started at me. She grabbed his arm and he stopped and stared at her for a moment before starting continuing to me.

"Father, I need your help." I said as he walked quickly toward me.

He stopped and looked at me as he stood in front of me and smacked me right across my face. My neck snapped to the side, burning instantaneously. His wife went back in the house immediately.

"How dare you come here?" He said to me. "You have disgraced me and you have disgraced your husband. Antonio called me last night and told me everything. You know we don't have a phone and the neighbor had to come and get me. He knows everything. Everyone knows everything!"

"Father this is Antonio's baby, please believe me." I pleaded with him.

"You need to leave now." He said.

65

I looked to the side beginning to raise my voice as I spoke to him.

"I have nowhere to go, father." I pleaded with him.

"You should have thought of that before you cheated on your husband." He retorted.

"I didn't!" I shouted, "Papi please!"

I hoped that this would get to him. I remembered calling him Papi when I was younger.

My father looked at me and shook his head before turning his back and walking away.

"Father, you owe me." I said.

He turned around and walked back over to me. His eyebrows rose with every step he took.

"I owe you nothing." He spat out quickly. "You have proven that you are a whore just like your mother was a whore."

I watched him with my mouth slightly ajar. I realized what a horrible man he was. He watched my expression for a moment before turning to walk back into his house. Commotion poured from the windows as his wife confronted him. I wiped my face and turned to walk away. I had no idea where to go but I walked slowly as I had begun to feel tired and hungry. I heard footsteps run up behind me and turned around to see Madrigal walking quickly toward me. Her gym shoes splashed as they caught in the mud.

"Here," she shouted out of breath as she approached me. She handed me a bag full of change and two bananas.

"I was saving the money for a car, but consider this a gift for my nephew." She said. "The bananas are from my mom."

She smiled at me. I smiled back, looking at her for the first time as my sister.

"Thank you." I said softly.

She hugged me, her eyes full of tears. She held me for several seconds before she turned and ran home. Well at least one person was on my side I thought to myself. I sat down on the side of the road for a few minutes, eating the bananas and rubbing my sore feet against each other. I decided I would walk to Elena's house. Her flight in should have landed last night. I stood up and began to walk toward her house.

After about an hour I arrived at the gas station near her house and used the payphone to dial her number with the change Madrigal had given me. Miguel answered the phone and hung up on me the second he heard my voice. I stood in shock momentarily and stared at the phone. I tried to remember Roberta's phone number with no success. I thought for a minute and then called Antonio. Maybe he would give me Roberta's number. The phone rang three times before he picked up.

"Bueno." Antonio said.

I immediately started speaking without knowing what to say.

"Baby, I need your help." I blurted out quickly.

He hung up on me and I stood for a long while, staring at the phone receiver. I put my hand on the glass of the phone booth and asked the lord to give me some kind of direction. I gazed at the scenery, the muddy river that flowed silently, separating our small town from the larger neighboring town where we could shop at. I felt as though my life was in total disarray. I stood observing the town for a few moments, before the steeple of the church caught my attention. I began to walk toward it.

I sighed as I walked. I would have to walk for at least an hour to get to the bridge that crossed the river. My feet were tired, but I began to rush. I needed to make it there before it became dark. I didn't have a clue as to what kind of wildlife came out at night and I wasn't about to find out.

There was something special about the church. It was the church that Antonio and I were married at. I would be able to sit down on a pew and rest for a while without having to worry about the people around me in the town or about the weather. I tightened my furry robe and sighed as I rubbed the sides of it. It had begun to cling to my pregnant belly and become uncomfortable in its wetness. I looked at the street signs, trying to remember how to get to the church. I knew that I would be fine after crossing the bridge. I started walking as fast as my legs would carry me. Finally I made it there. I opened the door and felt warmness surround me. I rubbed tiny rocks and sand that had stuck to the sides of my slippers from them before entering the building.

I walked over to a pew and sat down, quickly crossing my hand to my head, chin and either side of my face. My legs throbbed with pain. It felt like blood rushed through them immediately. I looked down at swollen feet that were now red and blistered. I sneezed three times in a row. I sat back in the pew and looked up at the huge portrait of Jesus on the cross and closed my eyes. I didn't mean to do it, but I fell into a deep sleep almost immediately. I tried to fight it at first, but then I told myself that I would just close my eyes for a minute. Minutes later, I found myself pulling my body to its side and stretching out on the pew.

I awoke nearly two hours later to find five nuns standing around me talking with one another. I sat up quickly, my stomach cramping up as I did so. I knew that they were talking about me and I felt terribly disrespectful for falling asleep in the church.

"Please sisters, I'm sorry for falling asleep here, but I had nowhere to go and I was so tired." I said as I held my hand out with the bag of change in it.

"This is all the money I have, but if you let me stay here, I can work for you or help you somehow." I said, to them with questioning eyes. "Please don't make me leave."

The nuns shook their heads and one took my hand in hers.

"I am Sister Rosa." She said to me, pausing as she spoke.

"This is Sister Maria, Sister Hilda, Sister LeiMei and Sister Madelyn," nodding at each as she went down the line. "We know who you are as well."

I smiled at them and they returned my smile with warm smiles.

"We cannot accept your money at this time." Sister Rosa continued. "We know what happened. We will let you stay with us, until everything has simmered down with your husband."

I nodded as tears fell from my face. I was happy that they were allowing me to stay and embarrassed at what they may have heard.

"If it makes you feel better to work, you can." Sister Rosa said. "In your condition, I'm not sure that you can handle it. The only requirement we have for you is that you study the word of God while you are with us."

I smiled at her and nodded. Sister Maria, the oldest of the nuns motioned for me to follow them, leading me down a hallway leading away from the sanctuary and up a short flight of stairs. The stairway was narrow and dark. At the top of the stairs there was a small room with a bed.

"You can stay here." Sister Rosa said, as she led me into the room. Sister Hilda the largest of the sisters handed me a white jogging suit and a new package of underwear I assumed she'd bought for herself. I thanked her and took my clothes off right away, trying to get into something warm and dry. Although the clothing was big on me, it felt incredibly comfortable.

"How far along are you?" Sister Rosa asked.

"Well I haven't been to the doctor yet, but I'm assuming three months or a little over three months." I replied.

Sister Rosa told the other nuns in Spanish and their eyebrows went up. I touched my stomach, feeling slightly embarrassed. I knew that I was really big for three months. Sister LeiMei and Sister Madelyn left the room brought me some soup and water. I thanked them and began to eat. Sister Rosa looked at my feet and then brought me some of her socks from her room.

"You'll need these." She said.

I thanked her, putting them on my swollen feet carefully and began to eat. When I was finished, they excused themselves and retreated to their rooms. I fell asleep on the bed, having horrible dreams the entire night. I was worried that I would have the baby alone. I felt incredibly scared. How was I going to care for this baby if Antonio wasn't going to be there to help me? I needed to get ahold of Roberta. My problem was that I didn't know her and Marcus's last name, only that it was different then Antonio's.

In the morning Sister Rosa came to wake me up and we ate oatmeal before going down to the Sunday Church service as it began. I sat down in the back of the sanctuary, feeling uncomfortable immediately as I looked around to hundreds of accusing eyes as the nuns proceeded to the front of the church. The church was crowded and many turned to look at me, whispering to each other as they did. I slumped down in my seat to avoid their gazes. I could feel the heat from everyone's glances on me. Those who sat remotely close to me got up to move to other already crowded sections of the church, leaving me easy to spot as I sat alone. I tried to listen to the priest as he spoke but it was impossible with everything that was going on around me.

I got up quietly and left the sanctuary, walking down the hallway and back to my room, where I could hear the priest's voice vaguely echoing through the hall. I found a mop bucket and some other cleaning supplies and begun cleaning our living quarters until church was over and the nuns returned to our quarters. Sister Rosa looked surprised to see me cleaning, but gave me an expression that told me that she understood why I left the sanctuary.

About half an hour passed before Sister LeiMei brought me lunch. I put down a scrub brush and walked over to thank her. Once again we were eating soup with a few crackers and juice. I couldn't complain. It was better than nothing at all. The food didn't fill me, but it stopped my stomach from rumbling.

That night I left the church and went to the closest payphone, determined to persuade Antonio to talk to me. I called Antonio at home. One of the maids picked up, putting the phone down to call him and then coming back to take a message. I heard him talking to her in the background, asking if it was me and then letting out an annoyed sigh. She slowly put the receiver down, after apologizing to me when I asked repeatedly to give the phone to him.

I breathed in and out for a minute and then called his cell phone, going straight into his voicemail.

"Antonio." I said slowly on the message. "Baby it's me. What I'm telling you is true. You have to believe me."

I paused, waiting as if he could hear me and might answer.

"Please. It's not possible for this baby to be from anyone else." I said. "You have to believe me."

I hung up the phone and paused, staring at the receiver as I set it on the hook. My heart was racing and I was filled with the feeling that I must prove myself. If I could just talk to him one more time, I was sure that he would understand. I called back several more times in a row and going straight into voice mail each time. Finally as I used the last of my change to dial again, I stood there staring at my reflection on the keypad.

"Antonio, this is the last of my last money." I said. "I swear I never cheated on you."

I breathed in, feeling difficulty speaking as I said each word.

"I'm staying in the church." I sighed and then pulled on the cord of the payphone. "The whole world hates me Antonio, I don't deserve this."

"I wish that I was dead right now." I looked around and noticed that a few people, who were walking by, stop to stare at me. I turned my body to them, speaking directly into the phone.

"You are the man that I love." I said quietly. "I love you more than anyone that I have ever met. More than I even love myself."

I stood staring out the window of the steaming hot phone booth.

"I'm scared Tony." I whispered.

I glanced around again as the people standing around the phone booth seemed to multiply.

"I'm so scared. I know how everything must have looked to you, but you have to trust me." I wiped my tears with the inside of my blouse.

"Please come and see me, Tony." I said. "I swear, I love you so much."

I paused again as the people around me spoke amongst themselves, laughing and shaking their heads. At that second the voicemail cut me off. I looked around at the people and slowly walked back to the church, avoiding making eye contact with any of them.

Chapter Four

For the next couple of months I spent my nights cleaning the church. During the day I retreated to my room to sleep, afraid of brushing shoulders with any of the local townspeople. I woke up for breakfast, lunch and dinner, staying awake only long enough to eat, before returning to sleep. Sister Rosa was the only nun who spoke fluent English. When she had a chance to talk to me she mentioned nothing of Antonio or of my pregnancy. Instead we talked about God and about my mother. One day she came to my room and asked me what I would do if I had the chance to go back to the night that my mother and I sat in the car.

"I would tell her to run the light." I replied without any hesitation. "I would tell her to drive away as fast as she could."

Sister Rosa saw tears begin to well in my eyes and quickly changed the subject. She turned our discussion to the bible and quizzed me on things that she asked me to read. She did this often over those two months. I felt that I knew the Bible from front to back before long. It was kind of weird for me at first, but soon things began to fall into place for me.

When I wasn't reading the Bible, my mind was set on Antonio. Despite my wish to see him, he never visited me. I couldn't help but to think of him as I fell asleep each morning as daylight streamed down the long hallway, pouring into my room. I felt distraught as I thought of Antonio. I often sat on the pews of the church without saying a word when I was supposed to be cleaning. I would just stare at the cross on the wall for hours.

One day when I was cleaning the church, I began to have trouble breathing. I disregarded the feeling, catching my breath moments later and kept scrubbing. Two weeks after the first incident, my breathing problems became worse. I suddenly began to feel like I couldn't get enough air and also began to have persistent pain in my abdomen. I stopped cleaning and would just lie in my bed the entire day. My skin felt like it had stretched to its capacity and I felt like the baby would burst right out of me at any moment. I didn't have time to think about Antonio as the pain began to get worse.

My ribs felt bruised and as if they were ready to snap from the pressure. Finally, a week later I could not move at all. I awoke one morning for breakfast with pain under my rib. I guessed it was my baby's foot. I tried to move it, but it jammed its foot in further further, causing more pain and a persistent pressure on my bladder. I moaned in pain loudly and Sister Rosa came running in from her room followed by the other nuns. I cried, telling her that I felt as though I would die from the pain, my face becoming so warm that sweat begun to pour from it. She quickly called for the other nuns and they tried having me move to a different position to help, but it only made the pain worse.

"I feel like I'm going to die." I whined to Sister Rosa.

She turned to talk to tell the other nuns in Spanish. Sister Maria and Sister Hilda shook their heads nervously and left the room.

"They are going to tell the priest." Sister Maria explained. "You need to go to the doctor and it's time that we get your husband involved."

I shook my head frantically at her. I forgot about the pain, now an overwhelming fear came over me in worrying over seeing Antonio again. I would rather die than have to sit before him in pain. I felt embarrassment come over me and began to panic. Within seconds I was having trouble breathing and struggled to get my words out to her as she rubbed my back and tried to help calm me.

"No, you can't call him!" I blurted out through my heavy breathing. "Tell them they can't call him."

The nuns returned and spoke to Sister Rosa. Pain shot through my body and I moaned so loud that I couldn't hear what they were saying as the pressure increased. I grabbed my pillow and moved to my side, moaning for at least two minutes straight. My eyes fluttered to the back of my head as I tried to find something in the room to focus on. Finally as quickly as it started, the pain stopped. I glanced at Sister Rosa as she sat down next to me, wiping the sweat from my face.

"They are actually going to call your father in law since your husband has moved and they do not know the number." Sister Rosa said as I looked up at her for reassurance.

"That bastard," I muttered to myself as I held the base of my stomach for relief, the pain beginning again.

Sister LeiMei and Sister Madelyn brought me pillows from their rooms and put them on the sides of me, which unbelievably helped to comfort me. Sister Rosa rubbed my sweaty head until the pain stopped and I fell into a deep sleep. When my eyes fluttered open again, Antonio Salvador and Elena were in my room staring down at me. The pain started again as I opened my eyes and moaned. Elena ran over and I grabbed onto her hand. When the pain stopped she hugged me, holding me in her arms for a long moment as she rubbed my back. After her hug she lifted me up to a sitting position.

This only made the pain return and worsen as I quickly lay back against the pillows.

I felt so utterly horrible I closed my eyes and moaned tears streaming from my face. I opened them a second later and realized that Antonio was in the room also. He stared smugly at me without saying a word. Our eyes met and he quickly looked away. The panicking feeling started again and everything went black as I fell back against the pillows gasping for air. I regained my composure moments later as Elena fanned me with her wallet and Antonio Salvador tried to get a cup of water to my lips as he rubbed my shoulders with his free hand.

"Oh, thank God." Elena said. "You look so pale."

"Thanks." I managed to whisper before feeling more pain and grabbing her hand. I moaned in pain as I looked up at her.

"Elena my stomach hurts so much." I said through tears as she looked down at my stomach.

"Your belly is huge." She said, smiling nervously and glancing across the room at Antonio.

He raised his eyebrow at her and smirked as he straightened up and sat back against his chair. I wished that he hadn't seen me like this. My body felt as if it melted into my bed in humiliation.

"Do you feel like you are in labor?" Elena asked quietly rubbing my hand. Tears formed in her eyes as she waited for my response.

"I can't be." I quietly responded. "I'm only about six months pregnant."

Antonio choked on a laugh and my face immediately reddened. His father shot him a nasty look. I tried not to look at either of them. Elena helped me to sit up again and when I did I saw that Antonio, Gilbert and Marcus were all sitting in a corner of my tiny room. Antonio and my eyes met and I looked away as did he. I felt helpless and embarrassed.

"Let's get you out of here." Antonio Salvador said as he stood up.

Marcus came over and each went to either of my sides and lifted me, carrying me down the hall way, through the church and out to the car quickly. Elena ran alongside of them and as soon as we got to the car put big fluffy baby blue slippers on my swollen feet. Antonio walked stubbornly behind us with Gilbert. Antonio Salvador and Marcus set me down and Elena got into the back seat and helped me in.

"I've been looking all over for you." Elena quietly told me. "We all have. We felt so relieved when the Father called us this evening."

I tried to smile, but I felt so much sadness that my face wasn't cooperating with me. I wished that it was Antonio who was telling me this and I stared out the window at him as he approached the car. Our eyes met again, but he turned to Gilbert instead of coming to my side. Gilbert and Antonio exchanged looks and Antonio went to sit with him in the front of the car. Antonio Salvador climbed into the back of the car with Elena and me. Marcus followed as we pulled away in his own car. Elena asked me question after question as we drove, but I just cried and moaned in pain, shaking my head as if to tell her that I couldn't speak.

I felt stupid and uncomfortable being around them. I didn't feel like any of them were my family any more. I felt alone even though all of them surrounded me. Antonio Salvador rubbed my head and whispered encouraging things to me softly as we drove. Antonio turned and glared back at him coldly as if I disgusted him. A cold pain shot through my chest and I whimpered in pain.

"Everything's going to be okay." Antonio Salvador said to me over and over.

Elena rubbed my leg, not knowing what else to do. She asked Antonio to hand her his water bottle, which he did halfheartedly and lifted the water bottle to my chapped lips, trying to get me to drink some. Antonio sat smugly in the front seat of the car as water dripped down the side of my mouth. When we arrived at the hospital, Elena tried to check me into a hospital suite but Antonio told her that he would not be spending that kind of cash on a baby that wasn't his. Elena glared at him as if she wanted to kill him herself. I didn't say anything but felt a cold twinge of pain shoot through my neck and chest as I tried not to think of what he had just said.

"Have some respect for your wife." Antonio Salvador said to him sternly.

Antonio said nothing else and delayed at whatever it was that he was doing in an attempt to aggravate the situation. I gazed at him silently and was astonished that through all the pain that I was feeling and all the suffering that he had put me through, I still loved him. I wished that he was the one to hold me and to tell me that everything was going to be okay. I looked down at the slippers on my feet as tears fell from my face. My heart felt as if it had sunk into my stomach as I stood before them.

"We have a woman in labor here." Elena stormed off screaming. "We need a wheel chair."

Minutes later she returned with a wheelchair. Nurses stood in the hallway staring at us, focusing in on Antonio and me, as I stood uncomfortably in his presence. I had no doubt that they were looking for clues as their eyes studied our behavior. Meanwhile Elena was near tears. She glared at everyone around her as she walked right over and pushed Antonio to the reception desk.

"Antonio," she screamed. "Stop wasting time and get her checked in."

Antonio smiled at Elena and turned to the receptionist, showing her his expensive watch and beginning to flirt with her as I watched in horror. My face went white and I could feel my limbs go numb. I started to whimper and turned around to try to leave, letting go of Antonio Salvador's arm and walking past Marcus. Antonio Salvador rushed to my side as I nearly lost my balance.

"Get off me!" I screamed, as I freed myself from them and turned to walk away. "I'll have the baby in the street before I go into a room with him."

Gilbert and Marcus ran in front of me and blocked my way as I tried to leave the hospital.

"Sweetie," Marcus said. "You'll have the baby here, I promise you."

His eyes showed me sincerity in his word. I shook my head and he hugged me as if he was my own father and tried to comfort me. It felt good to be held in his arms. I almost felt that he was there to protect me. I allowed him to hold me for a moment and held him back, pushing my face against him and beginning to sob uncontrollably until I lost my breath. I pulled away and collapsed to my knees in front of him crying and moaning, while clutching my stomach. I could feel everyone starring at me in pity. The nurses, the receptionist, even Antonio looked down at me as I cried on the filthy hospital floor. Marcus kneeled over and wrapped his arm around my waist.

"It'll be okay sweetie." He said quietly.

I looked up at him and through my tears I could see that his eyes were also watering. I allowed him to hold me and pull me to my feet. Elena brought the wheel chair over and the three men helped me in. I put my dead down and felt ashamed, closing my eyes and trying to take deep breaths to overcome my anxiety. I lowered shoulders, feeling as though everyone in the room was staring at me.

"I swear boy, if I wasn't your Uncle, I would beat your ass." I heard Marcus say to Antonio as they wheeled me by him.

I opened my eyes for a second to see Antonio slowly come to walk by my side. It was surprising to me to hear Marcus talk this way to Antonio, as he was the one that Antonio respected the most. I wondered if it was just the fact that they were seeing me now in this position that was bringing them to support me. Where had all of them been? I knew that Elena had said they looked for me, but no one came to the church, in spite of everyone in town knowing that I was there.

I was checked into a room with someone else who was in labor. I looked around the room in horror as she screamed and tried to push her baby out. A nurse quickly pulled back a curtain to separate her from us. I looked around the room, feeling scared as I gulped down my saliva. The paint on the walls was peeling and the picture frames on the wall looked like they hadn't been dusted in months. Antonio was definitely not going to spend any money on my care. That much was apparent.

The woman screaming in Labor next to me scared me so much that for a minute I didn't even feel my own pain. My hands began to tremble in fear as I glanced back at Elena. A doctor entered the room shaking his head and studying a clipboard. Antonio Salvador and Marcus moved as far to the side of the room as possible to make space for him to pass.

"This is the first time you are seeing a doctor." The doctor said condescendingly to me when he saw the size of my stomach.

I nodded nervously.

"The baby may come out with one eye." The doctor said warningly. "No prenatal care, definitely not a good sign."

"Maybe he will look like his father then." Antonio muttered just loud enough for me to hear and laughing.

The doctor glanced over at him but said nothing as he approached me, covering me with a sheet and removing my pants from below it. My legs trembled hard as I felt his hands move them apart. Antonio Salvador, Antonio, Marcus and Elena all stayed in the room but looked away as the doctor began to examine me. At this point, I didn't care if the entire town was there. I just wanted to be out of pain. My legs began to shake so hard that the doctor had to stop and ask Antonio to hold one of them. He put a hand on my leg to hold it still as the doctor began to check my insides.

I looked away from both of them and cried and moaned in pain. I felt like the doctor was going to pull the baby out his self. As he reached inside of me, I felt painful sensations shoot through my body. He removed his hand, pulling off his gloves and tossed them into the trash. He exchanged glances with Antonio and began to press down in different spots on my stomach as he listened to it with his stethoscope. Antonio still stood at my feet, holding my leg for a moment before breaking away from me.

"Dios Mio," the doctor said over and over.

He put his stethoscope away and shook his head over and over. I was so scared of what he was going to say, that I could hardly breathe. The lady next to me was screaming louder now as another doctor came into the room and examined her. My doctor began to pace the room. Suddenly the room was silent and the other doctor left the room. My doctor turned to a nurse and asked her to hand him a syringe filled with liquid that was across the room on a table.

"What is it? What's happening?" I asked.

The doctor said nothing to me. He took out a pad of paper and began scribbling notes and mumbling to himself. The nurse stood at his side and handed him the syringe as soon as he was done writing. The doctor gave me a shot of whatever it was and soon I felt more comfortable. He pulled a blanket up to my waist and turned to the nurse.

"See what other rooms are available." He said quietly to her.

She quickly left the room, nodding her head as if she knew what was going on. Antonio and Elena exchanged confused glances.

"I gave her a shot of Tocolytic, to stop the labor." The doctor said to the rest of us.

Everyone in the room looked surprised. I felt woozy from the shot and did not open my mouth to question him.

"Why are you stopping the labor Doctor?" Elena asked.

The doctor shook his head angrily and muttered something in Spanish. I felt hot and laid my head back on the bed, as Elena began to stroke my hair. I didn't care what was going on, I thought I was dying at this point. I wondered if Antonio would leave my body somewhere on the side of the road or if I would have a headstone of some sort. Antonio Salvador asked the doctor what the problem was, appearing to become very worried. The doctor looked around the room at each person one by one, and then looked down at me.

"The problem is that even I believed the rumors." The doctor finally said. "I should know better."

"Excuse me." Elena blurted out. "What does that mean?"

The doctor shook his head snapping himself back to reality as he stared at Elena in shock, realizing that the rest of us had no idea as to what he was talking about. I noticed several nurses gather in the hallway outside of the door and begin to whisper with one another as they tried to discretely peak in the room. He shook his head again and finally began to speak.

"Pre-labor." He explained and then said simply, "We needed to stop it."

"Two." He said, holding two of his fingers up and glancing around the room to observe everyone's faces. He noticed the nurses outside the door and begun to talk very quietly.

"There are two babies." He said directly to Antonio.

"Two." He said again, making it evident that he was trying to get his point across as Antonio glanced over at me nervously.

I looked back at him for a moment closing my eyes, surrendering to Elena as she stroked my head. Now he knew that he was wrong. I could see it in his face. The fact that there were two babies in my stomach would explain a lot to everyone, including me. Now I knew why early on, when the babies first started moving, I felt as if I was being attacked. I had four tiny feet kicking me at once.

"There is a problem." The doctor said. "She is too thin."

I immediately opened my eyes, scared to death that the doctor was about to disclose horrible news. Everyone exchanged worried expressions. Antonio stood up and walked across the room, pushing his fingers through his curly hair. Marcus shut the door of the room. I could see the shadow of the woman's husband in the bed next to me sit up and lean toward us to eavesdrop on our conversation. The doctor huddled in toward Antonio and his father to continue the conversation.

"Her examination is telling me that she is right at about six months." The doctor said knowledgably. "This means of course that it's too soon to deliver the babies."

He clasped his hands together waiting for Antonio to respond and when he didn't the doctor began to pace the room. The doctor glanced over at Antonio Salvador and shook his head.

"We'll have to keep her here and monitor her health until she is ready to deliver." The doctor said. "Also, we want to keep those babies in as long as possible."

Antonio Salvador and Elena exchanged looks as the doctor spoke. The doctor walked across the room towards the door and turned to Elena this time.

"There will be no getting out of bed for her, no bathroom, nothing. Understood?" He asked Elena. "If those babies come out now they will have health problems for sure. This wouldn't have happened if she had been taken care of and nourished properly."

"One last thing, I don't want her to have any stress whatsoever." The doctor looked directly at Antonio as he spoke. "Perhaps you shouldn't be in the room with her if you are still deliberating on what your position as a husband is."

With that comment the doctor walked out of the room, apparently very upset. Antonio nodded as the doctor walked past him, as if to thank him, but said nothing. Elena quickly jumped up and reached for her cell phone as she walked out of the room.

"Make sure that she gets her own suite." Elena said angrily to Antonio.

Elena made a quick phone call in the hallway outside of the door before returning and Antonio Salvador wiped sweat from his head. Everyone stood quietly for moments before saying anything.

"I knew I was going to be a grandpa again." Antonio Salvador finally said. Elena smiled at him and hugged him. Antonio left the room with Gilbert and did not return that night. I was taken minutes later to a beautiful hospital room. Elena followed as a nurse wheeled me down the hallway to my new room. The room hand long flowing curtains that nearly touched the floor, it was clean and smelled as if the floor had just been mopped. I noticed that the sheets were soft, rather than hard and scratchy like the ones in the room that I had just been in as I climbed into the bed.

There was an overhead TV and mirrored walls on one side of the room. The paint in the room was a calming shade of yellow. I nervously laid back in the bed as I felt like I was suddenly in a dream. I was ready for someone to pull the bed from beneath me, or for everyone around me to disappear. Soon after I was settled into my new room, Marcus and Antonio Salvador entered the room. Antonio Salvador carried a bouquet of flowers and a couple of balloons, while Marcus carried a bag full of tacos that he had bought from a vendor stationed outside of the hospital.

"I know this doesn't make up for what you've been through, but we just wanted to let you know that we are all here for you." Marcus said as he bent down to kiss my forehead.

I tried a smile, but it didn't work. My lips quivered and I didn't end up saying anything. They turned on the television for me and took turns kissing my forehead before saying their goodbyes. Elena and I were alone in the room and she chattered on about different things to ease the tension. Elena stayed with me the whole night and I was glad about that because I was tired of being alone.

A nurse came in and started me on an IV. She took my blood pressure and told Elena that it was low and that they would be giving me plenty of salty foods, in order to elevate it. Elena looked toward the mirrors in the room shook her head. I noticed that she glanced at the mirrors throughout the night. The next morning she had to return to her family but said she would be back to stay with me every night until the babies were born. I nodded as she kissed my cheek and left the room.

For the next three weeks my room was flooded with family. Everyone took turns spending time with me, so that I was never alone, everyone except for Antonio. The thing that I enjoyed most about Antonio Salvador's visits was that he always found something interesting to bring for me to eat. He looked just like an older version of Antonio. He had his same build and hairstyle. The only difference was that he had gray in his hair and deep wrinkles around his eyes.

"How is Antonio?" I muttered to him one morning quietly as I ate a doughnut.

I couldn't help asking him. I felt empty inside, as I waited for him to respond. As much as I despised Antonio, I wished that he could be there with me, feeling the babies move or just simply holding my hand. Antonio Salvador looked over at me and smiled. He touched my cheek lightly.

"Antonio is not the best person in the world." He said to me in a low tone, "but I know that he deeply regrets everything that he did to hurt you." I smiled and nodded at him.

"Would you like to see him?" He asked, reaching for his cell phone.

I immediately shook my head, despite the fact that I longed for his touch.

That night when Elena came to visit me, I poured out my feelings to her. Elena could see the pain in my eyes. She told me that Antonio was at the hospital almost every evening when she came to visit. I shook my head in disbelief. She glanced over helplessly at the mirrors.

"He is, he's just too afraid to come inside the room." She explained lightly, studying my face for a reaction.

I didn't say anything. I didn't believe her. I lay silently until I fell asleep. The next morning I saw Gilbert walk past my room while talking on his cell phone. I began to wish that Antonio would come in and talk to me. I stared at the mirrors and shuttered as I looked at my reflection. I could see how alone I was. You could see it in my face. I wanted to have Antonio there with me in spite of everything that he had put me through.

Gilbert began to bring me balloons and flowers every day which he didn't hesitate to tell me were from Antonio. He made some attempt to cheer me up, by telling me odd jokes that he had found on the internet. I could see that he was uncomfortable and I felt uncomfortable as well. I hardly knew him. He was this huge, rock of a man with a tiny head placed on top of his broad shoulders. I didn't know what to say to him. One day, as Gilbert left he handed me a folded up piece of paper with Antonio's phone number listed on it. I stared at it for a long while, not saying a word to him as he left.

I decided that I did want to talk to Antonio, but didn't know how I was to go about starting a conversation with him. I asked the nurse to bring me the phone that night. I lay in bed staring at it for hours. I even picked up the receiver and hung it up quickly without actually dialing his number.

"Why do I feel like this?" I said aloud when no one was in the room.

I began to feel like a horrible person, I rehearsed what I wanted to say to Antonio out loud as I lie alone in my room. I began to feel really bad because I had never spoken to the babies inside of me or rarely even reached down to touch my belly, unless I was in pain. I couldn't understand how I felt more alone than ever and I had these two lives inside of me. I suddenly felt that I had to move, that I had to get up and walk around.

I painfully moved myself out of the bed and felt the babies fall against my bladder. I clutched my stomach as I moved slowly, walking out of my room and down the hallway. I suddenly stopped when I noticed Gilbert talking to a nurse at the end of the hall. I scanned the other side of the hallway, but all was quiet. I grabbed my stomach and attempted to carry it down the hall. As I passed the room next to mine Antonio came out.

"What are you doing?" He asked. "You need to be in your room taking it easy."

He quickly came to my side and attempted to put my arm over his shoulder.

"Why do you care so much?" I asked angrily.

I pushed myself into the room that he had just come out of, thinking I was going to find another pregnant woman or a beautiful nurse in the room with him. I proceeded inside, looked around and gasped. Antonio covered his face with one hand as I did. The room had a window that looked into my room. From this room you could see into every corner of my room as well as the entire bathroom. The room had a sofa and a table with a telephone and magazines galore.

"You've been watching me?" I asked softly.

"We thought you were suicidal." Antonio answered sternly.

He attempted to move me out of the room again. I pulled away from him, continuing to stare at my room. Footsteps pounded down the hallway toward us. Gilbert and two nurses came running in and Antonio shooed the nurses and their three inch heels out of the room.

"Con cuidado." One nurse said to him.

Antonio pulled me despite my struggle back out into the hallway and called for Gilbert who helped him bring me the next few footsteps back into my room. I was as huge as a house, but I tried to break away from their grasp. Neither one of them paid attention to me until after they had got me into the bed. Antonio turned to Gilbert and told him to leave.

I felt exhausted and lay back on my pillows. The babies began to move and kick like crazy as I pulled a light blanket over my stomach. Antonio looked down, noticing their movements and stared into my eyes. I blushed and looked away. I didn't know why I couldn't stop loving him, regardless of the way that he treated me. I looked up at him, as he continued to stare at me.

"Can I?" He asked.

I said nothing. I closed my eyes and soon I felt his hand on my stomach. I began to cry and I felt him wipe my tears with his free hand, rubbing my face softly as he did. The babies kicked harder and harder and soon I felt his head on

91

my stomach pressing down lightly as he rubbed my stomach with his cheek. My stomach began to feel wet and I opened my eyes for a second to see that he had tears pouring from his eyes. I closed my eyes and pushed him away. He stood up and caressed my shoulders.

"I'm sorry Liliana." He said. "I'm sorry for being the asshole that I am. I was wrong, I've always been wrong."

He stared at me for what felt like hours as he backed away from my bed. He brushed tears from his face as I restrained myself from reaching out to him.

"The truth is that you're the best thing that ever happened to me and I'm going to figure out how to make this work." He turned away from me, this time leaving the room.

I put rolled to my side, putting my hand over my face and began to sob. It's funny how someone who causes you so much pain also makes you feel so good I thought. His simple touch made me feel loved. Having this feeling for the first time in my life scared me. I was scared that someone was going to somehow take that feeling away. I leaned to my side, deep in thought. For the months of pain Antonio had caused me, I felt full of desire for him to touch and hold me again. I fell into a deep sleep, not wanting to wake up from a happy dream that I was having.

Chapter Five

I woke up hours later with a jump. The doctor was standing over me, getting ready to examine me with Antonio at his side. I held my hand up to try to stop them but Antonio signaled to the doctor to go on. Antonio smiled warmly down at me, but my eyes filled with furry in response. Antonio reached down and put his hand on my shoulder, as if to comfort me. I glanced up at him in disbelief, but did not ask him to remove it.

"Well you made it to your seventh month." The doctor said as he motioned for me to turn over and began to check me.

I felt uncomfortable as Antonio was staring directly at the doctor's hand as he entered me. I looked away, grimacing in pain. Antonio rubbed my arm, to try to comfort me.

"It's getting to be too hard on your body." The doctor said shaking his head, "if we wait any longer something bad may happen."

I glanced over at Antonio and he nodded at me in support.

"Will they be okay if you take them out now?" I asked.

The doctor shrugged his shoulders as he motioned to a nurse and inserted a drug into my IV to begin the labor. I wanted to stop him. I didn't think I was ready to be a mom.

"There's no way of telling until they're here." The doctor said.

Antonio went to the hallway and asked Gilbert to call Elena and his father. I was extremely frightened and began to tremble. Antonio came over to my side and rubbed my arm. I shook my head, but Antonio didn't leave. Before long, I wanted to yell to get him out of the room as I struggled in pain, but when I opened my mouth all I could do was moan. Antonio mistook it for me wanting him closer and came and put his hand on my shoulder.

A nurse came and put monitors on my stomach and sides and the room was filled with a beeping sound. I closed my eyes because I could not bear to look at Antonio. I grasped the metal bar at the side of my bed and rocked back and forth. My stomach felt like it was ripping apart slowly in every direction. My back throbbed in pain as I lay in bed trying to find a comfortable position. Gilbert was in the room, flipping channels on the television which was suddenly extremely annoying to me. I wanted to kill him as I glared across the room without speaking. Antonio began reading a book out loud to me in attempt to comfort me and I lay quietly listening to him for about two minutes.

"Will you shut the hell up?" I finally said, mustering all the strength in my body. I glared at Antonio and then at Gilbert, my eyes nearly popping out of their sockets. The voice that came out of my mouth was not my own but reflected the sweltering anger within me.

Antonio closed the book and nodded at Gilbert to leave the room. Gilbert smiled at me, turned the television off and went out to the waiting area. Hard pain pressed against my back and I tried to lift my body as it did, but couldn't and laid back instead, tears pouring from my face. I thought I was going to die.

As the pain ceased momentarily, I glanced over at Antonio. I could tell that he didn't know what to do as he sat staring at me. I stared at the hands on the clock, feeling as though my labor had already taken an eternity. The pain began to grow stronger and I reached over and held the metal bar at the side of my bed with both hands, whispering to Antonio to call the doctor. Antonio pressed a button at the side of the bed, just as Elena entered the room and immediately came to my side. A nurse dashed in just after Elena and explained that she would examine me, but no sooner did she lift my sheet then she left the room, muttering something about going to get the doctor.

More pain raced across my body as I pushed Elena away and reached for the bar, this time raising myself to a seated position and nearly falling back in pain. Antonio came to my side and began to rub my back. I glanced back at him, shooting him a deadly glare just as the doctor walked in. The doctor instructed everyone in the room to put on gowns and I looked around helplessly at them as they did.

The contractions were increasing in pain. I felt like there was no break in between each one. I lay moaning in the bed, wishing that this was a dream and that I would soon wake up. Soon the doctor instructed me to push and ordered that I push in a certain direction. I didn't realize that I had already been pushing and felt like my insides were about to burst open. The nurses put my legs into metal brackets. My legs began to tremble uncontrollably as I looked down at them.

"Push," the doctor said.

I did, and then he said it again and again. Aggravation began to grow inside of me because I felt like we were getting nowhere with the pushing. I was scared because an increasing amount of pain raced through my body as I looked up at Antonio and Elena. As I stared at them, I began to feel defeated.

"I can't. I don't want to do this anymore." I shouted out at them.

I began to shake my head and moan. Antonio grabbed my shoulder and looked me deeply in the eye.

"You can." Antonio said. "This is going to be over soon."

He stared at me, his beautiful eyes full of sincerity. The same beautiful eyes that I had fallen in love with and the same eyes that I couldn't bear to look at, the day he came to pick me up from the church. I blinked and the hospital room went out of focus. I didn't know what had come over me. Perhaps it was the eerie feel of his touch or the sincere look in his eyes. Whatever it was, I gathered all of my strength and punched him right in his eye.

Everyone in the room gasped. He stepped back and grasped his eye, not so much in pain, but more so in shock. I felt good for a moment. Elena's jaw dropped and she shot him an expression that made him smile. He knew that he had better take it and shook his head before coming back to my side, this time standing slightly further away. That content moment didn't last long as pain ripped through my body seconds later. I reached down and held onto my stomach with both hands.

I felt like a brick was passing through me as my bones pulled apart. I swore that I felt each one of them move, as they made way for the babies head. I grabbed Antonio's hand because it was the first thing I saw and squeezed down on it hard as my body was ripped apart. I felt like the babies head was stuck inside of me breaking me from inside out. Antonio tried to quickly glance down to see it, but I grabbed him around his neck with my free hand and pulled him closer and closer as I experienced overwhelming pain. The doctors told me not to push until I had another contraction. Tears streamed from my eyes and I swore at them before closing my eyes and releasing Antonio from my grasp.

I heard Antonio's father come into the room. Sweat dripped from my head as I felt Elena's soft touch on my arm. Without warning I felt extreme pressure inside of me. I couldn't control it and soon I heard everyone praising God as I felt the baby's head rip out of my body. The doctor and the nurses prepared themselves for the baby, gathering in closer around the base of my legs. There was some relief and soon afterward I gave one small push and the baby's body slid out.

I could feel its slimy body lying between my legs. It felt as though I had just given birth to an alien. My legs began to shake uncontrollably as the baby began to cry.

"It's a boy!" The doctor said.

Everyone cheered in excitement. I felt no joy. I felt like a creature was lying between my legs and couldn't wait for them to move it. Elena wiped sweat from my forehead as she stood over me smiling. Antonio obstructed my view of her, putting his hideous face over me to get my attention.

"Don't you want to see your baby?" Antonio said to me.

I pretended to fall asleep as I listened to the commotion in the room. I pressed my eyes together hard until I knew they had taken the baby away. Antonio shook me gently a couple times, but I actually was exhausted and unintentionally fell into a deep sleep. I dreamt of nothing but darkness as I heard the voices around me. Antonio Salvador told Antonio over and over again how much the baby looked like him. I suddenly felt a depression came over me, more so than I had ever felt in my life. I had entered my own dominion and felt antagonism building inside of me as I listened to everyone discussing how adorable the baby was.

Suddenly I opened my eyes, feeling a giant shove come from inside of me. I screamed as the next baby tried to push its way out on its own. The doctor and everyone else ran to my side, leaving the first baby in the nurse's care. That was my first glimpse of my first son. I could tell even from the distance I was at, that the baby looked like Antonio. I closed my eyes and pushed as hard as I could to get this baby out. The baby moved with great force through my body. I opened my eyes as the head came out and I could see the back of its head between my legs as the doctor told me to push.

I felt disgusted and fell back on the bed giving up. Everyone stared at me as if they were appalled by my reaction. The doctor ordered me to push and I shook my head angrily at him. I became angry as I glanced around at the rest of the so called family in the room. My emotions were approaching ferocious levels and I didn't know how to control them.

"I'm done." I said flatly to everyone in the room. "If you want the baby then you take it out."

The doctor glanced at the nurses before attempting to do just as I instructed and pull the baby out of me. The nurses simultaneously grabbed ahold of each of my legs, pushing them back to the sides and forcing me to push.

"Another boy!" The doctor exclaimed seconds later.

"The babies are beautiful." Antonio said as he leaned in over me and kissed my forehead.

I groaned. I felt rage burning inside of me. My eyes were weak and fluttered closed. I opened them again slightly to see him standing beside me waiting for a response.

"They look like you." I replied, meaning it more as an insult than as a compliment.

He smiled and beamed, glancing around the room. The doctor came to my side and said that he would help me push the placentas out as the room filled with the sound of two hollering babies. The afterbirth came out quickly and I was told that I was lucky because the two placentas had fused together. The nurses came to clean me up, as they commented on it being a miracle that I didn't rip myself open. I drifted into a very peaceful sleep as I lay watching everyone surround the babies in their incubators.

I began to dream of my mother and the night that she had been shot, the car ride with her was repetitive, playing over at least twenty times, until finally I heard the gunshot. It echoed in my dream and I woke up with a shake, realizing that an entire night had passed as I looked across the room at the window and the clock on the wall as it struck three o'clock in the morning.

The room was dark but the street lights poured in from a slightly opened blind. I sat up in the bed, not knowing where I was for a moment. I lay one hand on my stomach and it jiggled, bringing back memories of my pregnancy and my labor. I looked down it, realizing that it was empty. Suddenly I felt empty as well. I fought the feeling of loneliness as I sat alone looking around the dark hospital room. This was a new room. It was larger then the first room I was in and much nicer.

The room had flowers everywhere. I smiled and walked over to the door, peeking out and hoping to find Antonio or any other member of the family, but I saw no one except for one of the nurses who had guarded my mirrored room. I gasped and closed the door as she raced toward me. She opened it and handed me a robe, saying something quickly to me in Spanish, of which I only understood the word "Niño's".

I thought she asked me if I had delivered boys, and nodded my head. She motioned for me to follow her, holding her hand up to signal to me to walk slowly, glancing around, perhaps to find a wheel chair with no luck. I realized that she was taking me to the babies. I wanted to tell her that I didn't want to see them, but as I held my hand up, she led me quickly toward an elevator. She pressed the button to go to floor three and left my side the moment we got off. I glanced back at the elevator doors wanting to get back on, but curiosity overtook me as I stepped forward.

I had to at least look at my children, I told myself. I had carried them for seven months. I walked down the hallway, toward a window that stretched out along a full wall and saw a room full of babies. How would I know which ones were mine, I wondered? The room in front of me had at least thirty babies in it. I put my hand on the glass and peered in. I sighed as I glanced around the room until I noticed Gilbert standing at the entrance to the room. Then I saw them. Two tiny babies at his side lay in incubators. Even from this distance, I could tell that each resembled Antonio. I felt tears running down my cheeks as I removed my hand from the glass. They looked so small and innocent.

"Hi babies," I said quietly.

I felt a hand on my shoulder and turned to see Antonio. I stared at him for a moment before moving to the side. He grabbed me before I could run away and held me tightly as I squirmed, pushing my hands against his strong chest. I let out a sigh, when I realized that I couldn't get away.

"Get away from me!" I exclaimed.

He didn't move. I turned to see Gilbert look up and come to the door. Antonio nodded at him, indicating that everything was under control.

"I know their mine." Antonio said smiling down at me. "I've already had them tested. We can be a family again."

"You bastard!" I screamed at him, fighting back tears. "Did you think that would make me happy?

He stood still, holding me for what felt like ten minutes without uttering a word. He stared deep into my eyes and I didn't look away. I didn't want to move at first because I felt weak and was afraid that I would fall over at any moment. My heart felt nothing but pain. Finally I had enough strength to push him away.

"Let me go." I said, trying to move my body away from his grasp.

"I love you." He said holding me tighter, "More now than ever before."

With that, I broke away, running from him until I found a stairwell. I ran inside and sat down burying my head in my knees as I cried into the echoes. As I cried, I looked around the stairwell beginning to feel out of focus and reached up to grasp the railing tightly. A doctor who was coming up the stairs stopped by me and looked at the hospital bracelet I wore on my wrist. The doctor helped me to my feet and with out saying a word he took me to my room.

I slowly stepped inside and locked the door behind me. The room began to spin and I staggered across the room and threw myself on the bed. Nurses came to knock on the door, followed by Antonio who pounded on the door seconds later. About five minutes passed and the door opened. I glanced at Antonio as he entered the room from the corner of my eye as he entered, sitting down in a chair near my bed. We remained silent. Antonio moved his mouth a few times as if he wanted to say something, but nothing came out.

I wanted to tell him that something was wrong as I watched him silently. The room continued to spin as I stared up at him. I opened and closed my eyes as I glanced at him, his face growing blurry as I did. A nurse came in to check on me, moments later grasping her chest and hitting the alarm button on the side of the bed. Antonio stood up and came to my side immediately, glancing around the room as if to ask what was wrong. A few other nurses came in followed by a doctor within seconds. Antonio looked around nervously as the room was suddenly filled with the hospital staff.

"What's wrong?" Antonio asked a nurse.

She said nothing to him. The doctor began asking me odd questions like my name, my birthday, how old I was. I tried to look up and answer him, but as I did, my head felt light and I dropped it slowly to its side.

"What's wrong with my wife?" Antonio yelled at anyone who was listening.

Antonio stared at me when no one answered him and I attempted to raise my hand to reach out to him and felt it drop weakly to the pillow. The doctor looked up at Antonio as though just noticing he was in the room.

"She's hemorrhaging." He said calmly. "We're going to have to operate."

The nurses continued to clean me up. I tried to sit up and blacked out when I did.

When I woke up again, Antonio was at my side with the babies in car seats, ready to go. I pressed my eyes closed, hoping that he didn't notice that I was awake. I heard Elena begin talking on her cell phone nearby and suddenly I felt something cold on my forehead.

"She's been sleeping for a week straight." I heard her say. "The doctor said the best thing to do is to take her home."

I opened my eyes slowly. The doctor was standing above me taking my temperature. He looked over at Antonio, nodding his approval for them to take me home. Elena stood in the room holding a blue dress and smiling.

"Finally." She said to me. "I'll meet you at your house."

She walked over to the babies and kissed each of their hands. I felt groggy and annoyed that I was being rushed, upon waking up for the first time. There was a nurse sitting at the edge of my bed, as the doctor gathered his instruments together on a table nearby.

"How do you feel?" She asked slowly as if unsure of her words.

I felt annoyed, but nodded to indicate that I was okay.

"Tell her to get up slowly." The nurse said to Antonio.

Antonio told me to get up slowly and helped me out of the bed. His touch made me feel cold and withdrawn. The doctor and nurse left the room. I reluctantly put on the dress with Antonio watching. I slipped my feet into my fuzzy slippers and walked over to the babies, looking down at them without feeling any attachment.

"Where are you taking them?" I asked nonchalantly.

"Home." Antonio replied, a confused expression appearing on his face.

"Whose home?" I asked.

"Our home." He replied, angrily.

I shook my head as I stood looking down at the twins.

"I don't have a home." I said, stubbornly. "I'm certainly not going home with you."

"Where will you go then?" Antonio replied, becoming increasingly upset as he spoke.

"I'm going to take the boys and go back to America." I said.

He laughed immediately.

"Do you really think I'm going to let you leave the country with our children?" He shot back.

"Now they're yours?" I asked lightly, walking over to the twins.

He walked across the room and lifted their car seats, before I could try.

"Fine." I said my own anger building. "I will go back alone."

I began to walk toward the door.

"You can't do that Lily." He said loudly to me. "Like it or not, we are a family!"

"Now you think we're a family Antonio?" I spun around and said loudly. "Until when? Until someone else comes up with a crazy rumor and you disown me?"

"I have no family." I clenched my teeth and attempted to grab one of the car seats from him. "Where were you when I needed you Antonio? Did you think we were a family then?"

I turned and walked toward the door.

"Gilbert!" Antonio called out to him.

Gilbert appeared in the doorway and grabbed me as I tried to pass. A nurse who stood in the hallway turned her head helplessly.

"We are going to be a family whether you like it or not." Antonio said loudly, passing by us with the twins.

"I'm done playing games with you Liliana." He turned back and said. "You do not have a choice in this matter."

Gilbert shoved me apologetically into a wheelchair and wheeled me down the hallway following Antonio and the twins. I felt defeated as I sped by smiling hospital staff. The nurses said goodbye to me and many people we passed gave their congratulations. I glanced around when we made it outside, thinking that I could get away but Gilbert was one step ahead of me as I tried to get up, holding my shoulders and keeping me in the wheelchair. I watched as Antonio strapped the babies into the seats of his SUV, turning and grabbing my arm as he pulled me into the seat next to him with Gilberts help.

"Don't get me mad, Lily." Antonio said lightly as I sat beside him fuming. "You're only making this more difficult for yourself."

I had been through enough, I thought to myself. I hated everyone in the car and felt as if I had no way out. I wondered what catastrophe would happen next if I went home with Antonio. Antonio tried to stroke my arms but I moved my body as close to the window as possible. I had no desire for his touch. All that I felt was coldness when he touched me. Depression came over me as I stared out of the window. I debated throwing myself from the car while it was moving. I knew that psychologically something was wrong with me. I felt that death was the only answer to my situation.

Gilbert made turn after turn as we drove, into the mountains and into the jungle. Antonio had moved, I thought to myself. Finally we stopped in front of a huge mansion, bigger then Elena's. Everyone got out of the car. I hesitated in my seat, but Gilbert came around to my side and helped me lower myself to the ground. The temperature was different here. I could see more mountains in the distance as I stared at the house. The mountains looked different here because we up above the other houses, still not high enough where it was too cold.

The yard had beautiful flowers and a huge fountain. The driveway wound around the fountain, with small hedges separating it from the house. Birds sung their songs around us, as if they were welcoming me home. I stepped back as I stood admiring the white stone walls at the entrance of the home, losing balance and grabbing on to Antonio by accident.

"It's breathtaking isn't it?" He asked me. "I've been building it since before we were married. I wanted it to be a surprise."

I gasped without knowing what to say. I wondered what he would have done with it if I hadn't returned home with him. My attention immediately went back to the house. In front of me there were marble steps, leading up to two double doors surrounded by pillars. The grass stretched out for as far as my eye could see in either direction. As I gazed around, I noticed that there were quite a few cars parked in the circular driveway. I sighed, realizing that we had company. Antonio led me toward the house. As I stepped on to the first stair, I looked down at by soft slippers and paused. They felt weird as I pressed them against the hard marble steps.

Gilbert carried both of the babies in their car seats while Antonio walked up the stairs beside me. I held his arm reluctantly as we walked up the stairs. I felt weak, this was the only reason that I allowed him to lead me, I told myself.

Before we arrived at the top Elena flung open the door to greet us. I tried to smile, but only half of a smile spread across my face. Regardless of my expression, her attention was focused on Gilbert and the babies.

"Let me see my nephew's." She exclaimed while smiling.

I felt invisible as she admired them. I glanced down at them and could see that they both had their eyes open. I immediately looked away, not bending down or trying to touch them. I caught Antonio watching me from the corner of my eye. He seemed to be disappointed with my reaction to them, but I felt nothing but grief instead of feeling any type of happiness. How could I not want to see my own babies, I wondered to myself?

Antonio quickly motioned for Gilbert to take the babies inside. I continued to hold Antonio's arm as we walked into a large foyer. I looked around the room, immediately noticing a magnificent double staircase and a beautiful chandelier overhead. Antonio looked at me and smiled.

"All of this is for you." He said, smiling as if he meant it.

I glanced at him, feeling confused and upset. He looked away when I didn't smile at him or engage in his happiness. I hoped that he knew that having this house didn't change what I felt about him. I felt betrayed by not only him but also by his family. An overwhelming feeling of depression came over me as I stood before him. Suddenly at least twenty of his friends and family members walked into the foyer to greet us. I was suddenly more devastated than I had been moments earlier. There before the crowd was Blanca, at her side the pretty blonde woman that I had seen Antonio leave with the day he kicked me out.

Everyone began talking and huddling around the twins as I stood in shock. My face went pale and I released Antonio's arm from my grip. I wanted to scream at the blonde woman to stay away from my children, but I couldn't pull the words from my mouth. Elena and Antonio glanced at me just in time to see my look of horror. I backed up three steps, feeling outraged. I was humiliated and had to get out of there.

I turned and dashed out the door down the steps, toward the big black fence in a slow dizzy run. Memories haunted me as I ran. I heard Antonio's voice as he told me to leave the house when he had come home from his business trip. I heard Sister Rosa reading the Bible with me, and heard the sister's talking as they had the day they called Antonio to come and pick me up. When I made it to the fence, I shook it, pleading with the guards to let me leave. They pulled me away from the fence as Antonio approached, looking helplessly at them and at me.

"What are you doing?" Antonio yelled at me grabbing me from the guards. "We have guests that came to congratulate you."

I looked back at the mansion and at everyone as they gathered on the front steps. I moved my arm quickly throwing his arm away from my body.

"What do you think I'm doing?" I yelled back. "You left me with nothing Antonio, nothing. Now your sancha is here the moment I return home. How dare you!"

I stood stiffly as tears streamed from my face in anger and frustration. I debated on climbing the fence in an attempt to get away from everyone, but decided that I didn't have the energy or the courage to bother trying.

"What do you want?" Antonio screamed.

Chills went through my body as he spoke.

"Do you want me to ask her to leave?" He said as he calmed himself down.

"No I want to leave." I shouted back at him, choking on my words as I attempted to calm myself. "You have the nerve to have her here, in what is supposed to be our house?"

"Her?" Antonio asked. "What are you talking about, you're crazy? She is just my assistant."

Antonio looked toward the house his eyes meeting the eyes of the blonde standing next to his mother as he stared. She immediately looked away, crossing her arms as if she felt uncomfortable.

"I saw you kiss her the morning that you kicked me out Antonio." I replied calmly. "You drove right by me while I sat at the gate and kissed her in the back of the limousine."

Our eyes met and for a moment he seemed apologetic as he stood before me.

"She actually has the nerve to stand in my house and to greet my children." I said under my breath, holding my hands to my face.

Everything was suddenly so quiet that I was sure the entire crowd had heard me. Antonio grabbed my hand and began to speak fiercely to me as he glanced back at the crowd.

"Get back in there if you care about your family." He said in a low voice, as if it were a command.

I pulled my hand from his and with all the strength and anger that was building in my body I slapped him across his face. Our company gasped in disbelief as I turned and began walking across the grass. I had no idea where I was going, but I knew that I had to get away from him.

"No one cared about them or about me while they were inside of me." I replied fiercely, stopping momentarily and turning to look back at him.

"I wished that I was dead Antonio, I still do." I said loudly. "I refuse to go back to feeling like I am nothing and to continue overlooking all of your affairs."

Antonio's lip quivered as he looked at me. He looked pathetic as he stood there. I felt a sense of accomplishment despite the feelings of devastation.

"When did you ever stop calling me Tony?" He replied softly. "I never meant to hurt you. I'm so sorry that I did."

I wanted to throw myself into his arms and sob. I still loved him, but there was no way that I was going to give him any satisfaction in once again having his way. Instead I chose to turn and walk away from him. I walked quickly toward a garden at the side of the house.

"Tony." Blanca called from the stairs.

I saw him turn and walk back to the house from the corner of my eye. Commotion sounded from the stairs as I walked. I could distinctly hear Elena yell at the blonde to leave before she killed her herself. I continued walking in spite of the commotion and found a bench in the garden to sit down on. As I sat there, I stared down at my swollen feet. I could feel the cold walls of the church in my imagination as the feeling of hopelessness came over me.

I stared blankly into the water of a small pond in the distance as I wondered what had become of my life. I wished my mother was there to hold me. She would be able to make all of my problems to go away. If my father had been a good father and had been there for me just once when I needed him, I knew in my mind that I wouldn't be in this predicament. Above all, I wished that Antonio had been the man that I thought he was when I married him. The man he presented himself to be.

I began to cry as I sat alone on the cold stone bench. A feeling came over me that scared me. I felt a deep anger building inside of me, trying to get out. I wondered how my mother had gotten over my father. Had it taken her a while to forget him? Did he hurt her so much that she forgot of him instantaneously? I remembered the nuns and knew that somehow God would help to lead me in the right direction.

"Show me the right path." I said softly to myself.

It began to rain after what felt like twenty minutes past. I didn't move. I stayed seated on the bench, wiping the rain from my forehead as it fell and washed away my tears.

Chapter Six

Elena came to get me moments after the rain began to fall. Though I wanted to be alone, I felt grateful for her company. She stood staring at me for a minute before sitting down beside me. She put her arm around me as we sat in the rain.

"I'm sorry that I wasn't there for you Lily." She said softly, "but I'm here for you now, if you'll let me be."

I turned to her and fell into her open arms, sobbing without holding back.

"I want my mother." I said as I buried my face into her shoulder. "I want to go home with my mother. This is not my home."

My nose began to run as I looked up at her. I noticed that Antonio was silently standing in the background.

"Everyone is in the dining room." Elena said quietly, her voice trembling as she spoke. "Won't you at least come in and let me take you to your room so that you can get some rest?"

I sat quietly, finally nodding. Antonio stepped forward, but she shot him a scared expression that made him stop in his tracks. She held me around my waist and led me back toward the house. The doors echoed as they closed behind us. Antonio followed quietly at a distance.

Elena motioned toward a long double staircase, and told me that my room was at the top as she walked past them. Before I felt any confusion she took me to a closet at the bottom of the stairway which I learned was actually an elevator. As we got in, I noticed Antonio going up the stairs with Gilbert and talking under his breath. When we got to the room, Elena asked me if I wanted to shower, but I shook my head. She helped me take off my clothes and put dry ones on.

I walked over to the bed and laid down on it. I felt its softness, as I stretched my body out and tried to relax. As I lay back, I noticed Antonio watching us from a room across the hall and asked Elena to close the door. She reluctantly did and seconds later a nurse knocked on the door before coming in to examine me.

"Would you like me to have the nanny bring in your children?" The nurse asked.

I shook my head.

"I'm not ready to see them." I replied quietly.

The nurse exchanged glances with Elena.

"You don't want to see your babies?" The nurse asked.

Elena touched her arm but said nothing.

"No." I responded halfheartedly.

"Are you feeling okay?" The nurse asked, pulling out a breast pump from her bag and popping a battery inside. "Open your blouse."

"No." I replied quickly.

"Your children need to be nourished." The nurse said.

"I'll do it myself." I replied.

"Very well." She replied, leaving the pump with Elena and asking that she be sure I fill up two bottles.

Elena nodded, but did not look pleased. Was I frustrating her, I wondered? Why did that make me feel good, I questioned myself? Elena caught Antonio's eye as the nurse left and shook her head as the nurse closed the door behind herself. Elena began to talk to me but became aggravated when she talked and I stared blankly out the window without responding to her. She sat down in a chair beside me without saying anything for a while.

"Lily, I love you." She said, tears slowly falling from her cheeks as she waited a few minutes for a response.

When I said nothing she hugged me and told me to call her if I needed anything before quickly running out. I didn't even nod or turn my head to watch her leave. I lay on my bed, staring out of the window. I began to imagine my mother coming down from the sky with open arms, calling out to me to join her. Suddenly I was brought back to reality after feeling a hand on my leg and nearly jumping out of my skin. I turned to see Antonio, sitting at the foot of our bed, watching me.

I looked at him as his lips moved but heard no sounds coming out. Instead I imagined that I was hearing beautiful music and seeing musical notes float past my eyes. I smiled lightly as I watched them, laughing as they fell.

"Lily, Lily." He said and began to shake me.

"What?" I blurted out.

"Didn't you hear anything I just said?" Antonio asked.

"What you say is of no importance to me." I replied coldly, turning my gaze back on the window.

"Well then think about our children." Antonio responded gruffly. "You need to give them your milk so that they will be healthy."

I shook my head without looking at him.

"I can't." I said. "I don't have anything to give anyone."

A single teardrop fell from my left eye. Antonio stared at me with a confused expression.

"Here." Antonio said, handing me a glass of water. "Drink this. You'll feel better. You lost a lot of blood."

My hand shook as I took the glass from him. It began to shake so hard that he took the glass from me and held it to my lips.

"I feel so weak." I muttered.

He brushed the loose strands of hair from my face and continued to give me water until I had finished the glass. Then he sat me up and removed my breast from my blouse as if he were an expert. I looked away, feeling lost within my own soul. He pumped the milk for me as I whined in pain. It felt like my breast was fighting not to be sucked up this tiny vacuum. My breast throbbed and tiny pains seared through it to the tip of my nipple. I looked down away from him as we sat together. When both bottles were full, I had to admit that my breasts felt better.

"That's all you need from me." I said to him, closing my robe. "Now get out."

I felt so exhausted that I turned my head and fell asleep within seconds, not waking up again until the next afternoon when Antonio and his mother came to my room.

"Wake up." Blanca said coldly as Antonio shook my leg lightly.

I opened my eyes but did not move. I was immediately annoyed with Antonio for allowing his mother into the room.

"Leave me alone." I said closing my eyes again.

"Wake up and take a shower." Blanca demanded. "The residents are starting to line up."

She walked across the room, raising the corner of her right lip as she spoke.

"They want to meet your new family." She snarled.

"I'm not going anywhere." I retorted.

I rolled back, pressing my eyes shut.

"Suddenly you consider us to be a family?" I muttered.

"Get your wife out of bed." Blanca said to Antonio harshly, leaving the room and slamming the door.

I opened my eyes slightly, noticing that breakfast had been sitting on a table near my bed. I closed my eyes. Antonio nudged me again and again until I opened my eyes.

"Look outside." He said pulling, my body up and pointing to the open curtains. "All these people came to see our family, which includes you."

I reluctantly sat up in bed and noticed that there was a long line of people waiting outside the gate. I didn't want to disappoint anyone, despite of how horrible as I felt. I sighed and reluctantly lowered my feet to the floor.

"Is your girlfriend going to be joining our family today, or are you waiting to bring her back again after you fool me into thinking everything is okay again?" I asked nonchalantly as I stood up at the side of the bed.

Antonio gave me a dirty look.

"What happened was a mistake." Antonio said as he came to my side to help me walk to the bathroom. "That was months ago and I apologized."

"Marrying you was a mistake." I replied briskly. Antonio bit his lip as he glared at me.

"Okay I'll allow you to vent for a while, but eventually you will forgive me." He said.

"Why would I go and do something like that Antonio." I asked hatefully.

"Because I won't ever let you leave." He replied. "Eventually, you will see there is no other choice, but to forgive me.

I shrugged and looked away.

"I don't think that's going to happen, seeing as I hate you." I said under my breath, gritting my teeth.

I made sure I said it just loud enough so that he would hear me. He turned and glared at me like he wanted to hit me but immediately looked away. Elena knocked at the door a moment later, opening it herself as she stood holding a navy blue dress.

"Antonio bought you something to wear." She said lightly, sensing the thin air between us.

"More blue." I muttered to myself.

Antonio left the room and Elena helped me get dressed. She put makeup on me and insisted on fixing my hair.

"Can you try to smile?" She asked.

I gave her a fake smile, which seemed to please her and she lead me downstairs to the dining room. Everyone from our family was there, and was already seated for breakfast. I tried to turn away but Elena led me to an open chair on one end of the table facing Antonio. I did not let our eyes meet as I reluctantly sat down. I picked and played with my food as I sat there. Even if I felt hungry I wouldn't know where to begin.

"Eat something, we have a long day." Antonio said pointedly from across the table.

I gave him a stern look and put my fork down, reaching for my glass of orange juice, intending on only taking a sip, but instead finishing the small glass. I hadn't realized how thirsty I was. I reached for the pitcher of water and poured myself a glass, finishing it quickly as well. No one said a word, as they pretended they didn't notice that I had disobeyed Antonio's request.

"I don't know why you bother." Blanca muttered under her breath, loud enough for the entire table to hear.

Antonio shot her an expression that quieted her down while Antonio Salvador gazed at her as if he was upset. Everyone else began to make quiet conversation among themselves.

"Would you say there are about a hundred people here?" Antonio suddenly asked, glancing from Marcus to his father.

"If not more." Marcus replied, after taking his last bite of eggs. "The line goes on down the street."

A maid entered the room to let Antonio know that the photographer had arrived. He motioned for everyone to get up and the photographer suggested that we all head to the living room. The photographer sat Antonio and I on a brown leather sofa which was positioned over a beautiful oriental rug. I sighed again, glancing around at all of the family members who stood in the room around us watching. I couldn't help feeling reluctant to sit next to Antonio but I became nervous as the nanny came over and brought me one of the babies.

"Do we have to do this today?" I asked Antonio under my breath.

He pretended not to hear me as he stood up to take the other twin from Elena. The nanny stood in front of me with the baby and finally handed him to me when I realized that there was no way to get out of it. He was wrapped in a receiving blanket and I looked down just long enough to see that he was sleeping before I looked away. Blanca shook her head as she whispered to Roberta. Roberta began whispering to Elena soon afterward. I knew that she was asking what was wrong with me, but I didn't care about what anyone else had to say about me. I couldn't help how I felt. The two looked so much like Antonio that I could not look at the babies tiny features without feeling the same hatred that I did toward his father.

Antonio looked disappointed, but nudged me to point out the features that they had in common and different from each other. He went on to tell me that they even had two different attitudes as the baby he was holding began to yawn. I sat listlessly, paying more attention to the photographer as he set the rest of the family up around us. I knew that the way that I was feeling wasn't normal. I had never heard of a mother that didn't want to be around her newborn.

Despite everyone that was standing around me I felt like I was falling deep into my own world. I felt like I was dead even though I knew I was very much alive. The photographer took a few different pictures and then said he wanted to take a picture of Antonio and me together with the babies and then with each of us alone with them. I sighed, a very loud uncomfortable sigh when it was my turn and did not smile for any of the pictures. When I was told to look down at them for a picture, I looked down, but instead my eyes drifted across the room to Antonio, who watched me with a sad look on his face. I felt out of place, like I didn't belong there.

The photographer repositioned us as the villagers started coming in. They came in one family at a time, as directed by Blanca, the matriarch of this event. They posed for pictures with us and Antonio thanked them for coming and bringing their blessings to our family. I sat still without saying a word to them. I was a new mother and felt like I was holding someone else's children. I glanced around the room, ready for someone to take the two boys back, as I held them in either arm as they slept. How was it possible that both of them looked so much like Antonio, I asked myself? I glanced at Antonio who sat next to me smiling at a visitor. I felt angry suddenly, like something clicked inside me and realized that I had to get away from everyone that second.

"Can someone take them please?" I said right in front of a guest as the photographer snapped a picture.

Antonio took them from me immediately and I walked quickly into the kitchen. Elena came in after me and the cook that was there took out a tray of appetizers out to our guests. I put my head in my hands and leaned against the counter. Elena rubbed my shoulders.

"I don't know what's wrong with me." I said quietly to her.

"It will pass." She said, rubbing my back.

"No it won't." I said to her, looking her square in the eye. "I was a bad wife and now I'm a bad mother."

"No Lily, you're a great everything." Elena said, reaching over to try to hug me as tears formed in her eyes.

I heard the door close, but saw nobody enter.

"No Elena." I replied softly. "You are a great everything. I can't even look at my own children and love them or feel some kind of an attachment toward them."

"Some mothers feel that way at first." Elena said softly, rubbing my back.

"Do they feel like they are dead every minute of the day also?" I asked, breaking into tears.

Elena nodded as she stared helplessly at me.

"I'm sure that they do." She said softly. "Whatever you are feeling is natural. Marriages are not easy, that doesn't make you a bad wife and no one can ever tell you what you should feel as a mother."

She hugged me and pulled me back out to greet more guests after I calmed down a bit. As we entered the room, she left my side and went over to Antonio, whispering something into his ear. Antonio smiled at me, though his eyes showed a twinge of sadness. He continued to hold the babies, without offering one to me as I sat beside him. I held a tissue tightly in my hand in the event of another breakdown. I noticed Blanca eying me furiously from across the room; I folded my hands in my lap and returned her expression.

After an hour the last guests were announced and I looked up to see my half-sister Madrigal. I immediately stood up and hugged her tightly. She blushed and beamed at the same time. She brought three of her friends from the neighborhood, who promptly greeted me.

"Let me hold my nephews." She said forcefully to Antonio.

Madrigal sat down in my spot and Antonio put both boys in her arms. Her words caused me to crack a smile as I watched her holding them. This sent the photographer into frenzy mode. He shot pictures quickly as if he had waited for my smile the entire day. I felt for those short few moments that everything was going to be okay.

Elena and I looked over at Blanca as she cleared her throat from across the room. Blanca shot Elena a horrible expression. I knew that it was because she considered my sister to be low class and couldn't stand the fact that she was holding her grandsons.

"Mom, why don't you ask Papi to take you home?" Elena asked. "You look really tired?"

Blanca took the hint and left the room as Madrigal and her friends swooned over the babies. Antonio stood up, letting the other girls sit down around her and watched me happily, walking toward me and coming from behind me, placing both of his arms around my waist. A shiver went through my body as I stood before him helplessly. It was not a shiver of joy. It was me fighting the urge to push him away in front of my sister.

The photographer saw the great photo opportunity and shot a few pictures, as I stood with an awkward smile, observing Madrigal and her friends. Antonio took every moment that they were there as an opportunity to be close to me. He continuously kissed the side of my face, knowing that I was happy that I finally had a member of my own family to support me. I looked on as the three of Madrigal's friends spoke to Elena. When they finally decided to leave, they made it a point to congratulate me and hug me and give Antonio a dirty look as they passed him walking toward the door.

"Come back anytime." I said to Madrigal.

I didn't want her to leave, because I knew that when she was gone, my happiness was over. When the door closed silently behind her, I broke away from Antonio and went back to our room. I pulled the curtains shut to block out as much sunlight as possible and looked through the drawers to find something comfortable to change back into before climbing into the bed. I felt better after seeing my sister, but I still was not myself. I had no desire to be around Antonio or the twins.

A month passed and I still lay in my room withdrawn from the world around me. Antonio woke me up to tell me that he would be out in back having a meeting if I needed him. I lay silently in bed when he left. Antonio had begun having all of his meetings at the house. I knew that he did it so that I would always know where he was at. Elena knocked at the door lightly shortly after he left, coming in quickly and shutting the door behind her. In either hand she carried stacks of magazines.

"Maybe you can read these?" She said.

I forced a smile, getting out of bed and walking over to her to go through them.

"Thank you." I muttered.

"Well you look a little better anyway." Elena said.

I looked up at her and saw that her eyes stared back at me in an apologetic manner.

"You know, I kind of do feel a little better." I said quickly. "Not towards Antonio, but toward life in general."

Elena's eyes brightened, she smiled at me.

"How do you feel toward your babies?" She asked.

I looked down.

"Not any better yet." I replied sadly.

She nodded and walked toward the closet.

"Have you been in here?" She asked.

"No." I replied silently.

The truth was Antonio laid out my clothes for me every morning, regardless of the fact that I never got up to get dressed. I had no desire to move about the house or even to go downstairs to eat.

"Come and check it out, it's huge!" She exclaimed.

I walked over reluctantly. For the first time I walked into my closet and it appeared to be a single closet door in my room, opened into another large room, lined with shelves. On one side of the room were all of Antonio's clothes and on another side were all of my clothes. There was a loveseat in the middle of the room and two dressing rooms, just like at the stores. All of my clothes were organized not only by type but also by color.

"Whoa." Elena gasped, turning to me and smiling as she walked around the room, touching everything. "I never thought that I'd say this, but you've got more clothes then me."

I smiled at her momentarily before Antonio appeared at the door. Elena quietly excused herself as Miguel called for her from the hallway. My body trembled in resentment as she walked away. I was angry with Antonio for intruding on my time with Elena.

"Lily, you haven't been outside at all today, have you?" Antonio asked.

"Is that a joke?" I asked Antonio.

"No it is not a joke, this is serious, Lily." Antonio responded.

"Not on the balcony, or anywhere outside?" Antonio asked.

I shook my head. Antonio gazed at me with angry eyes for a moment and then beginning to pace the room again. He ran his right hand through his dark curly hair. I looked away immediately as my mind filled with mixed emotions for him. How I loved his hair and his eyes, especially when they looked heated and angry, as they did now.

"Were you worried that I caught you out there with the blonde again?" I asked.

Antonio suddenly looked surprised and walked over to me, taking my hands in his.

"I'm sorry you feel that way Lily, but it's not true." He said. "I realize how badly I treated you and I am very sorry for that. The girl that was here when you came home is gone now. There is nothing to worry about."

"What do you mean she is gone now?" I asked him.

"I mean she is gone." Antonio said reluctantly. "She died. Drove right off the mountain after leaving here the night you came home." Antonio said, without feeling as he glanced down at me. "Uncle Marcus was driving behind her and saw the whole thing."

My body shuttered. I may not have known the woman, but death was not something I wished on anyone. I immediately pulled my hands away from him and looked up at Antonio to study his expression. His face showed no emotion, which confused me.

"She wasn't anything to me." He said. "Hasn't been for a while. We dated long before I met you. My mother brought her over that night to help comfort me. She worked as my assistant for a while. Nothing happened, other than that kiss that you saw."

I sat and stared at him.

"You work from home most of the time Antonio." I said. "Do you mean that she assisted you with something here?" I stood up and paced the room, holding my hand to my head, feeling a headache coming on. "Who is it going to be next?" I asked. "First a redhead, then a blonde, maybe you better go brunette."

Antonio smirked as he watched me.

"There will never be anyone else again." Antonio said. "I was young and stupid."

He paused as he waited for my reaction. When I said nothing, he went on.

"There will be only you from this point forward." He said.

I put my hand to my head as he spoke.

"I wish that I could believe you." I said. "I wish that I could believe that we could ever be happy again."

My body was immediately filled with uncontrollable emotions.

"Get out of my room." I said.

My reaction surprised him. He sat quietly for a moment.

"This is our room." He replied firmly. "We will sleep here as husband and wife from now on."

I stared at him resentfully. He paced the room for a while, and suddenly left without warning. He left the door open as he walked across the hall to his study. I watched him until I finally fell asleep. He came to bed hours later, though he did not touch me. He and I lay with our backs to each other. For a second I wished that he would hold me. I wanted to turn around to see if his eyes were open, but didn't. I didn't want him to know that I so much as thought about him. I held my pillow as if I held him and buried my face into its soft layers.

The next four months went by repetitively. I had not broken my depression yet. Antonio would wake me up when he left in the morning and open the curtains, letting the sunlight in. As soon as I heard him leave, I would close the curtains and lay in darkness for most of the day. Elena and Roberta seemed worried about me. They came to say hello in the morning. They didn't stay long, leaving quickly to take the twins outside. I could hear the boys cooing and playing from my window.

Antonio checked on me throughout the day, staying in his study until very late, coming to bed after he thought that I was sleeping. He made a point of telling me when he was in the backyard having a meeting and if for some reason he had to leave the house he would ask me to come, even though I never would. When he wasn't doing business he was playing with the babies in their room or sitting in the study watching me quietly, waiting for me to come around and to call out for him.

I watched the twins from my bedroom window, when I was certain that no one could see me as the nanny and Elena took them into the water. They would splash around with confused looks on their faces at first as the water hit their chubby cheeks. I began to smile as I watched them play. Suddenly I felt like I was missing out, like I wanted to be part of their childhoods, but felt guilty that I had pushed them away for so long. I didn't know how to knock down the wall that I had put between myself and the boys.

Finally I saw an opportunity to get closer to them when Antonio was in his study with the door closed and they were outside at the pool. I snuck quietly outside to watch them. I giggled out loud as one of the babies laughed. Elena and the nanny heard me and called out to me. Elena smiled widely at me as I shielded my face from the sun with my hand. My heart skipped a beat as I took a step forward, gathering all of my courage and going over to them.

"Here," Elena said holding out one of the babies to me.

He wiggled his feet and laughed, as he reached out for me.

"I don't know what to do." I said shaking my head and blushing.

The nanny brought the other baby over to me and put it in my arms without waiting for me to respond. I felt his little body in my arms. I felt awkward holding the child, as I reminded myself that it was my son.

"Este es Carlos." The nanny said.

"Hi, Carlos." I said biting my lip and reached down and stroked his hair.

"This is Andres." Elena said, holding up the happy baby again, as he giggled.

Carlos eyed me as I stood staring at him, not knowing quite how to react to me. A tear fell from my face, as I realized it had been nearly six months since I had given birth to them. Before now, I didn't even know what my own children's names were. I was sure that Antonio told me, but that it was one of the times that I blocked out what he was saying.

"I'm such a bad mother." I said to the nanny as I held the baby at an arms distance, hoping she would take him back.

"No, no, no." The nanny said, pushing him toward my chest. "Que estabas esperando. Esperando el momento adecuado."

She nodded as she spoke. I knew that she told me that I was waiting for the right time. Her sincerity caused tears to fall quickly from my face as the baby began to cry, as if to sense my nervousness.

"Here, take him back." I said to the nanny, as the baby's face scrunched up.

She smiled, shaking her head as she walked away. I became nervous as she left the pool area completely. I glanced over at Elena, my eyes full of fear. Elena smiled at me encouragingly.

"Rock him." Elena said. "Like this."

She nodded at me to watch her. I tried to follow her lead and miraculously he stopped crying. He reached up for my mouth as he gazed up at me making little sounds as he muffled his cries systematically. We stared into each other's eyes for a few moments and then he fell asleep. The nanny came back out and took him from me as soon as I looked up, feeling much better that he was sleeping.

"Thank you." I said rubbing my arms uncomfortably.

"Same time, tomorrow?" Elena said to me as she got out of the pool.

I laughed and nodded. I looked up to see Antonio watching us from our bedroom window smiling. I smiled at him for a second before looking away, quickly following the nanny and Elena to the nursery. My heart beat nervously as we walked through the house and past the maids. They tried not to look surprised as they saw me walk by them and upstairs to the boy's room.

Their room was beautiful I thought to myself as we walked in. It was decorated to resemble a forest. I had never seen anything like it before. The walls had hand painted murals with birds that were detailed down to the folds of their feathers. The floorboards were newly stained a dark brown color, making it look as though we were trapped in a fairytale taking place in the forest. I glanced around and saw shelves full of clothing and at least thirty pairs of tiny shoes lined up on the top of the shelves.

"This is too much for the two of them to wear in their entire childhood." I said to Elena, who stood in the doorway drying her hair with a towel.

She smiled. I stood and watched the nanny as she delicately set them both in their crib, before going to an adjoining room and quietly closing the door behind her. She was an older woman. If I had to guess, I would say that she was in her sixties or seventies. I was glad that Antonio found an older woman to care for the boys.

"She was Antonio and my nanny when we were little." Elena said, as if she was reading my mind. "She has two children of her own, but they are grown and have moved away."

Elena walked with me to my room as she spoke. I caught Antonio watching us quietly from across the hall in his study.

"I have to take the girls home." She said, smirking. "Miguel is waiting."

I hugged her quickly, nodding. She smiled at me, her face glowing with happiness as she left. I went to my closet immediately and changed into a yellow summer dress. Perhaps the bright colors would cheer me up, I thought to myself. As I passed the mirror, I took a moment to gaze at myself. I shook my head as I stared at myself and quickly went downstairs to the dinner table. It was still early enough that the sunlight poured into the room.

The cook quickly began to pull out a meal that she prepared. Antonio soon joined me. He didn't utter a word as he sat down, our eyes only meeting briefly. It was our first time eating together since the breakfast that we had with the family when the twins and I came home. He sat across from me and smiled to himself as he tried not to look at me. I could tell that he wanted to talk to me as I glanced over at him in between bites, but he didn't speak. After dinner he went to his study and I read a book before going to sleep, feeling warm and happy inside.

Chapter Seven

A few nights went by and things were going increasingly better for me. I played more with the babies and they were starting to get to know me. I felt good about everything. Antonio sometimes came and sat nearby, watching me silently as he smiled to himself. I overheard Antonio on the phone one day while he was in his study and thought that I was sleeping, making it clear to his father that he was happy with my progress and wanted to make sure that certain family members kept their distance as I came out of my depression.

After hearing this, I became confused about my feelings toward Antonio. I knew that he had been incredibly cruel to me, but I knew from his actions over the past six months that he loved me and that he was trying to show that he changed. Tonight it was raining hard as I tried to sleep. The thunder grew louder and louder. I wondered if the babies were awake and went to their room. I found the nanny in a chair sleeping and the babies asleep in their cribs while sound effects played from small speakers on the wall, drowning out the noise from the thunder. I went back to our room and left the door open as I climbed into bed.

I could see Antonio in his study reading over paperwork with his glasses on. The thunder crashed again, harder than before and I called out to Antonio. He came to the room to see what was wrong.

"Antonio, can you stay with me for a while until I go to sleep?" I asked.

For a moment he looked confused, he glanced across the hall at his study and then nodded, closing the door and turning off the light. He lay down in the bed facing me, but not touching me. I stared into his eyes as we lay there without speaking to each other. All was quiet around us, except for the thunder. As I lay there staring at him in the darkness and breathed his scent in, I smiled lightly. Another thunder crashed loudly in the sky and I wrapped my arms around his sculpted back. He didn't know what do at first and reluctantly wrapped his strong arm around me. I felt well protected as I lay in his arms and nuzzled my nose into his chest, shaking slightly as a shiver went through my body.

"It's alright. I'm here." He said, caressing my back lightly.

I squeezed my body closer to his, glancing up at his broad chin. He leaned down and kissed me, I moved my face away immediately.

"I'm sorry, I won't do it again." He said, rubbing my back and straightening up, as he held me.

He let out a sigh as he lay next to me. I lay in his arms for a minute enjoying his touch, before finally looking up at him.

"Don't be." I said softly.

He looked down at me and we stared into each other's eyes for a moment. He put his hand to my cheek touching it softly as if to ask for permission. I nodded at him and he leaned down and kissed me again. First he kissed me softly, but he quickly changed hiss kiss to a hard and passionate one. I felt my body yearn for him as he caressed my back. I arched my body toward him, while we lay in a passionate kiss. I slowly reached down and stroked his manhood without stopping to think about what I was doing. I knew I wanted it, that I wanted him and that I wanted my life back.

He cupped my breasts with his hands, his touch filling me with ecstasy. He slowly began to strip my nightgown off, taking off his clothes as well between kisses. Finally he climbed on top of me. He suddenly stopped, looking at me again as if to ask me if I was sure. I stripped off my panties and wrapped my legs around him, pulling him into me as a response. He moaned a lustful moan as he slowly thrust his manhood inside of me, I moaned in pleasure loudly. I wrapped my hands around his neck and a second later he pushed my hands away, cupping my breasts in his hands and kissing them over and over.

He touched me and kissed me all over my body, making me feel good, in places that I had forgotten existed. I hit my climax again and again as he went on for what felt like hours. I held his back tightly and raised my head up to his chest in pleasure as I felt my insides growing hot from his penetration. He smiled for a moment and then opened his mouth and kissed me as he continuously thrust himself inside of me. I began to moan both in pleasure and in pain. Finally when he was done, he lay inside of me for what felt like an eternity without moving. He held me close and kissed my neck softly over and over again until I fell into a light sleep.

I felt him get up moments later and opened my eyes to see him go across the hall to the study. He left the door open so that I could see him sitting at his desk. He sat in his fitted boxer shorts trying to focus on his paperwork but didn't move at all. I knew he must be wondering what had just happened. I lay in bed watching him, feeling myself still twitching with desire for him more than it had before.

I lay in bed watching him for a while, wondering if I had done the right thing. Antonio seemed to be confused as he sat at his desk, and I wondered if I was as well. I had to be safe, I thought to myself. I could never find myself in a position again where I had nowhere to go. I made a vow to myself, that I would protect my future. One day I would go back to school and work on my education, but for now, I would save money in case Antonio ever turned on me again. I lay there thinking about what I could do in order to prepare myself, before falling asleep.

The next morning Miguel and Elena came by for breakfast with their son. Elena shot me a glance that told me that she noticed something was different between Antonio and me. I sat silently in my chair eating a spinach omelet, trying not to let our eyes meet. Antonio sat across the table from me with a smug look on his face as he spoke quietly with Miguel. Every few minutes he would glance over at me and smile as he spoke.

"Liliana, why don't we take the boys out to the stores or the zoo?" Elena said.

Miguel and Antonio laughed hysterically as I watched them.

"Honey, the zoo is nearly six hours away." Miguel said to Elena. "You would have to spend the night."

"I just thought it would be fun and Liliana needs to get out of the house." She replied as she glanced over at me for support.

I began to feel nervous. I didn't think that I could handle the twins outside of the house and besides that, I didn't know if I wanted to leave the house. I didn't feel like I was ready to leave. In an odd way, I felt safe within the walls of my house. I sat quietly eating my food as if I hadn't heard her bring up anything.

"I don't know." I responded to her finally as she intently gazed across the table.

"Antonio, make her come." Elena whined at him. "At least make her come to the store to go shopping. She needs some fresh air."

He shook his head, deep in thought as he lifted his hand to his face to move his curls to the side as he slowly looked up at me.

"Lily, I think it might be a good idea for you to get out of the house." He said to me seriously.

I stared across the table at for him with a blank expression, as I studied his face and eyes, which appeared sincere. I didn't know what to say. I honestly felt safer at home.

"Come on. We'll take the babies." Elena said insistently. "They'll love the change of scenery."

I looked down at my food as I thought about it.

"I guess it would be a good idea." I said softly.

"Yes!" Elena exclaimed. "Come on finish your food, I'll help you get ready."

Antonio smiled at me and picked up a newspaper to begin reading, while Miguel called Marcus to see if he was close so that they could begin their meeting. I ate quickly, beginning to wonder why they had so many meetings. Elena stood up and went into the kitchen. I smiled back nervously at Antonio as he moved the paper to glance quickly over at me. I looked down at my food. Was he thinking about last night, I wondered? He put the paper down and stood up and walked over to me and began to massage my shoulders. I jumped but I didn't stop him, it felt good to have him touching me again.

"Lily, I love you." He leaned over and whispered in my ear.

I sat quietly, not knowing how I should respond.

"Thank you." I finally said, getting up and starting up the stairs to go to our room and get ready.

"Wait." He called and I stopped without turning around.

"Here let me give you something. Buy whatever you want." He called up at me, walking up the stairs and handing me some money.

I didn't reach for it at first, but he took my hand and put the money into the palm of my hand, closing my fingers around it. I slowly looked at it and then tried to hand it back.

"This is too much." I said.

Antonio smiled at me and laughed as he walked down the stairs leaving me with a handful of bills.

"Spend it, however you want." He said. "Nothing is too much for my wife."

I stared at the money for a moment without moving. I shook my head and started for our room to get ready, as I remembered the promise that I had made myself the night before. I laid the money down on the bed and just stared at it for a while. I slowly put on a pair of tight jeans and white tee shirt. As I dressed, I thought about what to do with the money. I thought over the promise I made to myself the night before and stuffed half of the money Antonio had given me into one of the shoes in my closet. I felt nervous, but it was something that needed to be done.

Elena knocked at the door a second later and we left to go shopping, I decided to leave the twins with the nanny on my first trip out of the house. I was nervous enough as it was. I felt that when the gates closed behind us as we left, that I would never get back in. Elena took me to some of the most expensive stores in the area, where I bought nothing. After hours of window shopping and watching her make her own purchases, I asked her to take me to a department store across town, where I bought toys for the twins and two bottles of perfume for myself. She tried not to look confused and humored me as she went along with my idea. I could see the uncomfortable look on her face as we walked down the aisles of the department store with her son in a shopping cart.

When we were done shopping I still had money left over. We went to pick up her daughters at school and I noticed a bank next door to the school. I decided that the next time we picked up the girls I would try to break away from Elena for a few minutes and go to the bank to open up my own account. Elena dropped me off at home and Antonio walked out to the limo to help me with my bags. He shot Elena a strange look when he saw the department store bags. She smiled at him and told him that she would call him later.

The nanny came down the stairs seconds later with the twins and Antonio asked her to take the toys up to the twin's room, taking Andres from her and motioning for me to take Carlos. We went out to the backyard with the twins, who made happy noises upon being handed over to us. Carlos immediately tried to pull off my earring. I laughed as I pulled his tiny hand away from my ear. I followed Antonio to the area where he had his meetings. The area was shaded and comfortable. We sat silently for a moment as the babies squirmed and waved their hands around. I decided to sit Carlos down in the grass and he immediately grabbed at it, turning back to me as if he was scared when he felt it in his hand.

I picked him back up and held him tight while laughing at him. Antonio sat in his chair deep in thought as Andres drank a bottle of juice. Carlos reached for his bottle as well and the moment I put it to his mouth, Antonio turned to me with an odd expression on his face.

139

"Lily why did you buy things from those stores, we never shop there." Antonio asked me.

I sighed and sat silently for a moment.

"Antonio millions of people around here cannot even afford those stores. What makes the more expensive ones any better?" I asked.

I tried to hand him back the leftover money that I had, but he pushed my hand away.

"Keep it." He said gruffly.

I put it into my pocket without hesitation. We sat outside playing with the babies for awhile and the maid came to ask us if we wanted to have dinner inside or outside.

"Let's eat out here." I said to Antonio.

The maid didn't seem to be prepared for my answer. She looked to Antonio for approval. The nanny came to get the twins as they began to fall asleep and the maid waited for Antonio's response. I could tell that he was having second thoughts about eating outside, but he nodded and the maid brought us our food minutes later. She quickly went back into the house, as if she knew that Antonio would not react well to eating outside. I glanced over at Antonio who was obviously upset as he sat eating his steak without saying anything.

I remembered that Antonio was the type of person that liked things a certain way. He liked to eat dinner at the table, unless we were having a barbeque, he was old fashioned like that. He sank into his chair with his drink, a defeated expression appearing across his face as he chewed his last bites in silence. A maid came to take our plates when he was done. We sat outside for a little while afterward without saying a word. We both stared at the pool as if we were searching for the right words to say to each other.

I could tell that we were being watched by the staff. I knew that if I turned around I would see a room full of servants watching us from the kitchen. I stood up and went over to Antonio. He glanced up at me as I climbed on top of him and began to kiss him passionately. He pulled away and glanced at me, his eyes sparkling and a smile appearing on his face.

"I don't know what's come over you, but whatever it is, I like it." He said in the sexiest voice imaginable as he stroked my back.

I leaned over and sucked on his neck for a moment before getting up and going back to my chair, glancing at him with a naughty gaze in my eyes. Antonio sat open mouthed as he glanced back at me, seeming to be unsure of what had just happened. He adjusted himself and leaned back in the chair smiling as if he was the happiest man in the world. Gilbert came outside a moment later to tell Antonio he was going out for the night, if that was okay and motioned at one of the maids. Antonio stood up and nodded his head as he wrapped his arm around Gilbert's shoulder and whispered something to him.

Gilbert walked off and Antonio sat back down for a few minutes before taking my hand and walking me back toward the house. He paused as we walked through the doors, staring at me with a seductive gaze as I stopped and nodded, parting my lips as I felt my body fill with desire for him. He came at me and kissed me on the lips zealously, before leading me on to pass through the kitchen as I blushed. I could see the servants watching and smiling as we passed.

I wrapped my arm around his strong forearm and looked up at his dark eyes as he gazed down at me. I looked at them intently as there was something about them that held my focus on them. His eyes were the feature that I was most attracted to. There was something about them that made me feel as though I had known him forever. He walked me into our room and stayed with me without asking, following me in and closing the door behind him. We both lay down on the bed and he paused briefly before leaning over me and kissing every inch of my body. He made me feel good inside and out, putting his fingers inside of me and moving them around while kissing me passionately.

I allowed my body to convulse with pleasure beneath him, gazing up at his wry smile. Finally he slipped his manhood inside of me, without pausing to ask for permission. He pushed his way inside of me, holding me tightly in his arms and moving me in to positions that he never had before, thrusting himself violently inside of me and utilizing every inch of the bed. I flopped around like his ragdoll as he penetrated me but I enjoyed every minute of it. I moaned loudly as he turned me around and grabbed my breasts in one hand while holding my legs, bringing my rear toward him as he thrust himself into me again and again from behind. Finally there was a burst of warmth within me and he moaned as he held me tightly.

We were both covered in sweat as we fell into the comfort of our bed. Our naked bodies lay together, as I felt his manhood pulsating at my buttocks. That night he didn't get up to go to his study. He held me close to him the entire night. It felt good to lie inside his muscular arms. I turned around and rested my head against his hard chest and listened to him breath as I lay beside him. I felt fulfilled inside and though I couldn't forget the problems that we had, I felt like I was beginning to forgive him. He caressed my hair. His touch sent goose bumps up and down my body. I smiled, feeling comfortable and protected.

Chapter Eight

When I woke up the next morning it was past breakfast. Antonio was already at his meeting outside and I was a little upset that he didn't wake me up. I walked across the room and took a long hot shower before getting dressed. As I stood before the full length mirror in the closet, I noticed that I had hickeys all over my neck and chest. I put on a turtleneck with no sleeves and a pair of tight jeans before going downstairs to eat breakfast. On the table beside the food the maid brought me, were fresh roses in a vase on the table with a card that he must have scribbled his name on in the morning.

I quickly ate my food and headed up to the twin's room to check on them. The nanny greeted me as she sat on the floor with them showing them cards with colors and attempted to teach them how to pronounce the colors in Spanish as they looked around the room for some type of trouble to get into. I sat down on the floor with them, playing with them for a while before asking the nanny to come with me to take them for a swim. She nodded happily as she went to her own room and quickly got ready.

As soon as Antonio's meeting was over, the nanny and I went swimming in the pool. Antonio sat down on a lounge chair and watched us for a while as the boys laughed and splashed around. I motioned for him to join us but he shook his head and smiled. The babies were having a lot of fun splashing around the pool. Andres had the funniest little laugh and it would make us all laugh every time we heard him. He laughed for anything, throwing his hands up to splash himself.

Carlos was more serious. It took more than a little splashing to get him to smile. He never laughed he just cooed at us when he was happy. The babies were so chunky and cute, that I just wanted to kiss them and squeeze them every minute I was near them. We stayed in the water for about an hour before getting out lying under the sun for a while to dry off. The boys looked tired and the nanny lifted them up in her arms, saying that she was taking them to their room for a nap. One of the maids came out to help her as she walked back toward the house.

Antonio and I exchanged seductive glances momentarily before he stood up, coming to my lounge chair and kissing me.

"I messed up your neck, pretty bad, huh?" He asked as we broke away.

I hit him playfully in the chest.

"Yeah, what did you do that for?" I responded.

I had forgotten about all the hickeys on my neck and quickly covered them with a towel.

"Oh it's too late for that." He said, grabbing the towel and hitting me playfully with it.

I grabbed it back angrily and put it around my neck as I sulked.

"I'm sorry I couldn't help myself." He said, kissing me over and over until I laughed and pushed him away.

"Come on, Round Two, right here." He said playfully.

I laughed as I grinned at him.

"Get in the water with me." I said as I grabbed his hand and led him to the pool side.

I let his hand go as I jumped in the water. I stripped off my swimming suit and held it up at him, as he smiled and licked his lips.

"Come on." I yelled, throwing my swimming suit back at him as it hit his knees and fell to the ground. "Don't be a chicken."

He laughed at me, looking around quickly and stripping down to his boxers, throwing his clothing to a lounge chair. He stood there for a moment, watching me as I danced around the pool seductively, looking back at him as he stood, with the sunlight hitting every one of his toned muscles before he dove into the water. I laughed as his head popped up in front of me and he brushed his wet curls from his face.

"Take them off." I said pointing down at his boxers.

He shook his head at me, coming over to me and lifting my body to his.

"Our children swim in here." He said before kissing me and pulling me to him.

I shrugged, wrapped my legs around him and kissed him, as he pulled me under the water our lips locked in a kiss and immediately came up for air. I swam away from him as we emerged, telling him to catch me as we swam around the pool.

"Oh excuse me." I heard Gilbert say as he came out of nowhere and quickly walked away.

Antonio laughed and I gasped before laughing. He quickly came to my side pulling me close to him, to cover my body as I clung tightly to him in the water and he moved me to the side of the pool to reach over and grab my swimming suit, handing it to me as I quickly put it on in the water. We both got out of the pool, laughing and holding each other as we joked about Gilbert's face when he saw us.

"It's a good thing that wasn't my mother." He said loudly.

I laughed and he scooped me up in his arms carrying me to the house and up to our room, as I laughed and tried to get down. No matter how happy I was with him at that moment the dark memories managed to sneak back into my mind. I tried to push them out and went out of my way to appear happy as we bonded again. I felt the strong feelings that I had toward him growing, stronger then the feelings that I had for him before we were married. He acted as though he couldn't get enough of me. He spent every moment of his free time with me over the next two weeks, making me feel happy and loved.

I felt myself falling back into love with him, praying that this time everything would go smoothly. Despite my happiness, I was careful about letting anything bad happen to me again. I kept adding money that he gave me to spend to my money shoe when he wasn't in his study where he might catch me. I didn't want him to think that I didn't trust him. Our lives had welded themselves back together since I opened myself back up to him and I didn't want anything to tear us apart.

I waited for the opportunity when I could sneak away from Elena's daughter's school long enough to walk over to the bank and open up an account. The shoe was completely stuffed and I didn't want anything to happen to it, or for Antonio to catch a glimpse of it as he dressed. One day when Elena and the nanny were busy with the boys in the new playground that Antonio had built, I said that I would pick the girls up for her if she kept an eye on the twins.

She glanced at me suspiciously and I smiled reassuringly back at her, telling her that I needed a break from everyone for a while, so that I had a moment to think. Antonio was still in his meeting and I knew that I would be back before it was over. The playground was on the side of the house, so I could sneak back over to them, without him noticing that I had gone missing. She finally shrugged and nodded at me, happy to stay and enjoy our new toy with her son and the boys.

I dashed into the house and ran up to our room, grabbed the shoe, stuffed all of the money into a purse and ran downstairs to have Charles take me to pick up the girls. As we drove, I thought over what I would do and decided that I would run in the bank then back out to get the girls before Charles noticed anything. As soon as he pulled up to the school, I suggested that he go in a nearby café and get us all lunch so that we could eat something different while I went into the school to get the girls. I could tell that he didn't want to leave me alone, as he walked to the café, glancing back at me with a hesitant expression on his face.

I glanced down at my watch, knowing that they didn't get out for twenty minutes and quickly dashed to the bank, when I noticed his back turned from the car. My heart pounded loudly as I walked through the door and to the nearest teller. I had never opened a bank account before and asked the teller how to do it. She motioned for a banker to come over and he led me to a nearby desk. I quickly told him that I wanted to deposit the money into a bank account that only I would have access to. He raised his eyebrows at me.

"That's a lot of money." He said. "What are you planning to do with it?"

"I'm saving it to buy a nice surprise for my husband." I quickly answered him.

My heart pounded as I spoke. I felt as though he could see straight through me.

"It has to be a secret account." I said convincingly to him.

He nodded and proceeded to open the account for me, explaining to me how to deposit money and how everything worked. I looked at my watch. The girls should be walking out of the school by now. The process of him counting the money and depositing it into my new account took over half an hour. I nervously walked toward the limo after walking out of the bank. The school playground was empty and I knew that all of the children had already come out because I could still see a few of them walking down the block, toward their house.

When I got back to the car the girls were inside and so were the two bags of food that I had sent Charles for. I sighed, as I got in and grabbed my stomach telling him that I had been sick and had to run in to the bank to use the bathroom. He nodded at me and gazed at me through his sunglasses as if he believed what I told him. I hoped that he wouldn't mention anything to Antonio about me saying that I was sick. I stuffed the payment book from the bank into my shoe that night and hoped to God that Antonio wouldn't find it.

Elena and I went to the store just about every day. I ran into the bank once a week and she never asked me about it. I felt nervous doing it, but it was like a rush for me. I felt bad, but I knew I had to protect myself in case anything happened again. Two months of me depositing money passed without a hitch, until one morning that Miguel and Elena came over after breakfast with their children. She planned for us to go to a museum with all the kids and helped me get Carlos and Andres into their stroller. The nanny couldn't do that kind of walking, so I told her I would be fine and that she could stay at home. I put matching outfits on Carlos and Andres and smiled at how cute they looked. They looked at me with chubby faces cooing at me and motioning to their cousin as he wheeled alongside of them through the hallway.

Elena and her kids walked with me as I wheeled the twins to Antonio's study to say goodbye. I was excited to go to the city. I thought about visiting Madrigal while I was in town and mentioned it to Elena who agreed that it would be a good idea. I called Antonio's name as we turned the corner and walked into his study, but he didn't respond.

Antonio turned and looked at us as we walked in but then he turned his back on Elena and me talking angrily on the phone to somebody in Spanish. He lowered his voice slightly so that we would not hear what he was saying. Elena and I stood waiting for Antonio to get off the phone so that I could say goodbye, hoping that he would offer to give me more money that I might be able to stash. The twins sat in their stroller contently playing with toys that their Tia Elena had bought for them.

Suddenly Antonio slammed down the phone and turned to us. I could tell that he was upset, because he gritted his teeth together as he stared at me. I quickly blurted out that we were going into town and he nodded at me without saying anything. I nervously glanced at Elena and then decided to ask him if I could have a few dollars in case I needed to buy anything. With that he became enraged, throwing his chair back and walking over to me, slapping me hard across the face. He caught me off guard in doing this and the force threw me to the ground. I touched my face as it burned in pain and looked up in confusion at him.

"Antonio." Elena exclaimed before calling for the nanny and pushed my stroller and her kids out to the hallway without waiting for her to come.

"What is your problem?" I shouted at him.

There was furry brewing in his dark eyes. Elena put her hand on Antonio's chest as he started toward me.

"Get them out of here." He screamed at her.

Elena began moving the boys into the hallway. They had already begun screaming and crying. Elena looked back as the nanny and one of the maids quickly came to get them and take them outside.

"The bank called Lily!" Antonio screamed at the top of his lungs.

Miguel ran to Elena's side and attempted to pull her out of the room, but they both stopped as Antonio went on.

"What are you planning to do with all that money you've been taking from me?" Antonio hollered.

"Nothing." I said shaking as I spoke.

I knew I was wrong for not saying anything to him, but he was wrong for hitting me and for blowing this so far out of proportion.

"There's a lot of money in that account to be doing nothing with it Lily." Antonio screamed out again getting louder as he spoke. "For God sake, you could buy a car with that!"

Elena stood in the room silently, not knowing what to say or to do. She pulled at Antonio's arm to get him to calm down. Miguel walked across the room as if he wanted to leave, but not knowing what he should do he stood near the doorway in case he was needed. I lay still on the floor not looking at any of them. I felt embarrassed. I hadn't meant for Antonio to find out like this. I knew I had to tell him.

"I'm saving it Antonio." I replied as loudly as I could, my body shaking as I spoke.

Antonio smirked at me as I lay there looking up at him.

"Why would you be saving money?" Antonio screamed at me. "Are you planning to run away?"

"I'm saving it for the next time you decide to get rid of me." I said, tears coming to my face, putting my hand up to wipe them.

Elena glanced across the room at Miguel, who slowly took a seat in the sofa at the far end of the room.

"I don't want to be homeless again." I said. "I need to know that I will be able to support myself and the boys if you throw us out."

Antonio's face turned pale. His expression appeared as though I had just cut him with a knife. Antonio turned and paced the room for a moment. Elena's jaw dropped and then her face was filled with understanding as she frowned at Antonio. I knew that I had hit a weak spot for him. I felt embarrassed that he found out because it showed that I didn't trust him or have faith in our relationship, but at the same time, I didn't regret what I had done. Miguel slowly snuck out of the room without saying a word.

"How could you keep this a secret from me Lily?" He asked. "You could have come to me. You could have explained that this is what you felt that you needed to do."

I shook my head as he talked.

"Do you realize that everyone in town probably knew?" Antonio asked. "That's ridiculous anyway. If I wanted to get rid of you, you would know."

He let out half a laugh and glanced at Elena who immediately looked away.

"I didn't know the last time." I said as I pulled myself together, getting up from the floor and going back to our room feeling pain not only from my throbbing cheek but also throughout my entire body.

I lay down on my fluffy bedspread, immediately falling asleep, forgetting about going to the museum and about the money. When I opened my eyes that evening Antonio lay next to me watching me as I slept and smiled lightly at me as I woke up. I tried to get up, but he pulled me into his arms and hugged me tightly.

"I am so sorry." He whispered into my ear, "I am so sorry that I didn't come to you first, before jumping to conclusions when the man at the bank called."

I didn't look up at him as he spoke, although he paused as if he was waiting for me to answer him.

"Please forgive me." He said softly.

I pulled back and looked him in the eyes. His eyes, being my weakness, instantly made me melt.

"I'm sorry too, for not telling you." I replied. "I'm sorry for not trusting you, but I just can't right now."

He didn't release me from his grip.

"Why do I keep messing up our marriage Lily, what's wrong with me?" He asked.

"You're an asshole." I said simply to him, smiling and removing my shoulders from his grip. I went to the bathroom and sat down on the toilet and buried my face in my hands.

"Why can't I have a normal life?" I asked my feet quietly.

Just then there was a knock at the door and as I quickly came out of the bathroom. Antonio lay on the bed with our boys crawling around in their swim shorts on our bed. He laughed at little Andres who bounced on a pillow as he tried to stand and fell on his butt, crying. I ran over to Andres and held him in my arms, kissing his soft hair. Little Carlos got jealous and attempted to pry Andres from me. He pulled at Andres shorts and made grunting noises.

"They want you to take them swimming." Antonio said.

I stared at him blankly for a moment wondering how he could go from one extreme to another. Antonio apparently mistook this as an opportunity to caress me and grabbed me throwing me on the bed with little Andres. He pushed the kids away from me, throwing me back on the bed and kissed me all over. Both babies thought this was funny, laughing and crawling over to us and trying to climb on top of him.

"Stop." I said, trying to push him away.

He didn't listen and kissed me more, making funny noises as he went along, the boys laughing hysterically in the background.

"Don't be mad at me Lily." Antonio whispered.

The boys began to play with each other and the toys that they had on our bed.

I can't stand it when you're mad at me." He said as he shoved his tongue in my mouth, and cupped my breasts, making sure the twins weren't looking. I was embarrassed but finally managed to push Antonio off of me. He sat up, smiling at me and grabbed the boys as his defense. I tried to stay angry at him, but I couldn't. He had me under his spell, as a smile finally appeared on my face.

There was a knock at the door and I opened it to see Roberta in a swimming suit and skirt with a huge straw hat and sunglasses, looking absolutely ridiculous. I quickly ran over to her and hugged her and kissed her on her cheek. I felt incredibly excited as I hadn't seen her in a few weeks.

"Would you like to come with me to the pool?" She asked the boys. "Tio Marcus is downstairs waiting for us."

"They would." I replied. "I'll come too. I need to get ready though, I just woke up."

Roberta came into the room, smiling mischievously at Antonio and picked up a squealing boy in each arm.

"I'll meet you at the pool." She said as she walked toward the door.

"Oh and Antonio, Marcus wants to talk to you about something also." She turned back to us and said.

"Thanks Tia." He replied.

She smiled and I closed the door behind her. Antonio jumped up from the bed and took off his t-shirt.

"Well I better brush my teeth." He said as he left the room to go into our bathroom.

I reluctantly went into our closet and found my bathing suit to put on. I sat down on the sofa and began to strip off my clothes when my breasts were grabbed from behind. I jumped and turned to see Antonio, who covered my mouth softly for a second and then began to massage my shoulders.

I wanted to stop him, as I sat completely undressed on the sofa, but I said nothing because it felt so good. He continued for about two minutes and stepped around the side of the sofa revealing his buffed chest and strong hairy legs in boxer shorts. He looked so good at that moment, almost like a male swimsuit model. I felt uncomfortable and tried to cover my breasts and stomach, as I sat in the light. I was ashamed of all the stretch marks that I had from when I was pregnant with Andres and Carlos.

He knelt down before me and removed my hands from my stomach as he kissed my cheek and then my stomach, reaching around my back and grabbing my butt, pulling me forward toward him, where I had no choice, but to grab him or I would fall right on the floor.

He leaned me back, licking by breasts in circular motion, before ferociously beginning to suck on my hard nipples. I wanted to tell him to stop, but it felt so good, that I couldn't stop him if I wanted to. He raised my face, kissing me on my mouth and slipping his tongue into it, as he simultaneously slipped his enormous manhood into me. I moaned in pleasure as he leaned back and smiled at me. I clung to his strong arms as he began to work my body while watching my facial expressions change.

He didn't care for a moment that I had been mad at him minutes earlier and went on. I leaned my head from side to side in ecstasy as he penetrated me from within. I pushed my breasts out in front of him as I leaned back.

"Tony Stop." I said while moaning in pleasure. "Marcus is waiting for you."

"He can wait!" He said ferociously as he slung himself inward harder and harder.

I tilted my head back and he sucked on my neck as I moaned loudly, a rush of hotness suddenly shooting through me. Finally I felt a burst of warmth shoot into me as his eyes rolled back and he moaned, laying in me for a moment before slowly pulling himself out. I didn't look at him. I leaned forward and sat still for a moment.

"That was great, Lily." He said to me, quickly getting dressed and then kissing me on the head, leaving the room and going out to meet Marcus.

In Too Deep

I sat still for a moment before putting on my swimming suit which seemed to fit me tighter then ever. I looked at myself in the full length mirror and then found a wrap to cover myself as I went downstairs. I was still tired and felt fat. My body ached all over. I really didn't want to go swimming, but I didn't want to miss this opportunity to play with my little munchkins.

Roberta was already in the pool with the boys, each of them were seated in an inner tube and bouncing around in the water. I smiled and waved at them. Rosa quickly came out with a tray of food. I sat down at a table by the pool and ate some fruit and cheese. Antonio had a large wooden fence put in that separated the pool from the rest of the house, so that Antonio could have his meetings at the house and we could swim. He had even had another pool put in nearby for the boys to play in. This one would be for them as they started walking.

Roberta picked them up and took them to their pool, Carlos immediately squealed in delight. There was a water play center in the middle of their pool. They loved it already. Carolos sat on his butt moving from side to side splashing water without being held, while Andres had a grouchy expression as he was held in Roberta's arms. His face scrunched up like he was angry and he refused to have fun. It was funny how the boys were such opposites.

After I finished eating I sat for half an hour before getting into the pool with them. We played and the twins laughed at me as I jumped around trying to entertain them. As we played, everything suddenly became blurry and I became very dizzy. I mentioned it to Roberta and she gave me a worried glance.

"It has to be the sun." She said. "Let's get out. We'll go to the park and you can sit in the shade."

No sooner were we out of the water, then I leaned over and vomited all over the ground, clutching my stomach as it turned, and made me throw up more.

Roberta waved down the gardener, and asked him to call Antonio. I kneeled down on the ground by a pool chair, vomiting up more and more into the grass. Roberta looked nervously at me. She didn't know what to do. The boys were fussy because they wanted to go back into the water, as she held one in each arm. Everything blacked out for a moment around me, but I managed to pull myself onto the pool chair before everything came back into focus. I rubbed my eyes for a minute and saw Antonio and Gilbert followed by Marcus run over to the kid's pool where I sat. I reached for my towel and covered myself with it as the three approached. Antonio took one look at me and knelt immediately on his knees beside me.

"Baby, what's wrong?" He asked as he stroked my hair.

I shook my head and shrugged my shoulders.

"We'll take the boys." Marcus said. "You take care of your wife."

I tried to keep my eyes open but I felt wasted. I felt sweat dripping from my face, and my fingers trembled at my side. He put a glass of water to my mouth, but after I took a sip, I leaned to the side and began vomiting again. This time was worse. I began to get pains in my stomach.

"Close your eyes baby." Antonio said kissing my eyes.

I felt him lift me and carry me back to the house.

"Call the doctor," Antonio said to the nanny.

I shook my head as he carried me up the stairs.

"No, I'll be fine." I said quickly. "I think it's just the flu."

"Oh dear lord." The nanny said when she saw me and rushed to the phone.

Antonio took me up to our room and wiped my face with a damp cloth, as he spoke softly to me. It seemed like hours before the doctor got there. I was listless and dazed. I heard the doctor come in and ask Antonio what happened as he prepared to examine me. I heard a knock at the door and Elena entered a second later. I felt embarrassed. Why did this happen while we had company? Within seconds of me blacking out our entire family probably knew. I thought.

The doctor took my temperature and vitals and then said he would do a full exam. Before I knew it, he was feeling my insides and pressing down on my stomach. I looked to the side in embarrassment as Antonio and Elena watched. The doctor sat on the bed, smiling for a moment.

"She's fine, but I am going to recommend that she take it easy for a while." The doctor said. "Swimming is good, but maybe later in the day, when the sun is not so hot. A woman in your condition should relax a little."

Antonio and Elena looked at him in confusion and then Elena smiled.

"What's wrong with me then?" I muttered to the doctor.

"You're pregnant!" The doctor exclaimed.

I saw Antonio's eyes light up and Elena hugged and congratulated him.

"No." I wailed. "I can't be."

The doctor gave Antonio a stern look.

"I'll make house calls for you." The doctor said. "You make sure that she gets some rest and does not take in any stress."

"You heard the doctor Lily." Antonio said. "We can still have sex though, can't we?"

"Oh yes, that is fine." The doctor said as he laughed as he began to get his things together.

Elena came over to me and hugged me, brushing my hair off my sweaty face. I smiled at her as I sat in shock. I didn't know if I was ready for another child. The twins weren't even walking yet. Antonio walked off with the doctor, the doctor giving him instructions as they walked. Antonio came back into the room clapping his hands together a moment later.

"My baby is giving me another baby!" He sung out happily.

"Or two." Elena said smiling.

"Don't say that." I muttered, though wishing I had the energy to say more.

I didn't understand how one moment, I was perfectly fine and now I was overwhelmingly sick. Antonio and Elena acted as if they hadn't heard what I said as they talked excitedly with each other.

"Wow!" Elena exclaimed, smiling at me. "What if it's a girl?"

"I don't know, a girl would be nice, but I hope it's another boy." Antonio said.

Did they even remember that I was in the room I wondered? My eyes were blurry and I could hardly look at them. I was suddenly so tired that I felt like I was going to fall asleep at any moment.

"Everything is going to be so different Lily." Antonio leaned over and said. "You don't have anything to worry about Mamita."

A new name I thought to myself. I sat up and grabbed the wastebasket by the side of the bed just in time to throw up in it.

"I'm going to die." I plainly said to them. I felt like the room was spinning. I then fell back against my pillows and passed out.

Chapter Nine

The next four months went by quickly, however my life never followed course smoothly. After returning home from shopping with Elena one day, I noticed a commotion immediately upon walking into my living room. Antonio sat with Antonio Salvador, Miguel and Marcus. As Elena and I approached, the commotion immediately stopped and the men sat quietly as Antonio searched for something to say. I knew that something was wrong from the expressions that the four men had on their faces. I immediately went to sit down next to Antonio.

I held his hand in mine and looked into his dark eyes for an answer. He immediately looked away and glanced across the room at Elena. She shook her head and pressed her lips together, as if to show him that she hadn't said anything to me. I immediately grew frustrated. She was always the first to find out anything that was going on in the family.

"What is it?" I asked, as I felt my heart begin to pound with anticipation.

"Gilbert was shot today." Antonio finally said.

I instantaneously gasped.

"He's okay." Antonio said as he saw the worried expression appear on my face.

I sighed in relief, but the expressions on everyone else's faces were unchanged. Their expressions were those of regret. I knew that there was more to the story.

"Whoever shot him, didn't intend to kill him." Antonio said. "They were just intending to send a message."

"What kind of a message would they be trying to send?" I blurted out, knowing that I had interrupted his train of thought.

Antonio opened his mouth and closed it. He reached into his pocket and pulled out a pack of gum, opening it and sticking a piece into his mouth, without offering anyone else a piece.

Elena smiled at me nervously from across the room. We both knew that Antonio chewed gum only when he was stressed out. He did this ever since he quit smoking just after he graduated from college.

"It took place, shortly after you girls left." Marcus changed the subject quickly, noticing the concerned look on my face.

"The twins?" I immediately asked.

"They're fine." Antonio Salvador said. "The nanny was upstairs with them when it happened and Blanca is up there with them now."

"Oh my goodness." I exclaimed, still wondering what could have caused this.

"The shooter wouldn't have touched them if he had the chance." Miguel muttered, just loud enough for me to hear.

Elena shot him an expression that shut him up.

"We'll talk about everything another time." Antonio said plainly.

"Antonio, what else happened?" I immediately asked. "Should I be worried?"

He immediately glanced across the room at Miguel without saying a word. The expression that Antonio gave him scared me. Everyone in the room grew quiet.

"Absolutely not." Antonio said.

Miguel nodded his head in agreement, as his eyes remained locked in a stare with Antonio. Everyone stood up suddenly but no one said anything. I quickly stood up with them, feeling confused and afraid. I rubbed my belly, which was a good size now.

"I'll be in the guest room with your mom." Antonio Salvador said to Antonio as he quietly left the room.

Elena and Miguel left without saying much, as did Marcus, minutes later. I clung to Antonio as he led me up to our room. Blanca and Antonio Salvador spending the night with us told me that something was incredibly wrong. What was the sudden need to protect me and the boys?

Antonio spoke to me about other things that he had watched on the news as he led me up the stairs. I nodded at Antonio as he spoke, but I felt a chill go through my body. Something told me that whatever happened had to do with me. Everyone seemed to be acting differently toward me. Was it just that they didn't want me to know because I was pregnant? I decided that I didn't want to know. Whatever it was already scared me.

Antonio and I climbed into bed and I pulled the comforter up to my chest. Antonio held me close as I lay at his side. I listened to him breathing heavily, but I couldn't fall asleep. Within seconds he was snoring loudly and I tried to push our talk out of my mind. I lay still for what felt like hours before falling into a light sleep.

I woke up at exactly three o'clock in the morning. Moonlight poured in through our bedroom window and I could hear the sound of crickets buzzing outside. I slowly got out of bed and walked over to the bathroom. I gazed outside when I was finished and saw several more guards outside than usual. A couple of them focused their attention on the small street that we lived on, as two more walked back and forth through the grass.

I shook my head, wondering where Antonio had hired all these guards from. I glanced at Antonio as he slept in bed and decided that I needed to do something to take my mind off of what was going on outside. I climbed into bed and stripped off my clothes as I watched Antonio. I opened his pants and unbuttoned his shirt, going down on him for the first time ever.

"What are you doing?" He asked, waking up and pulling his manhood away from me.

"What do you think I'm doing?" I asked.

I climbed on top of him and pulled his mouth to mine. I kissed him lightly before going back down on him.

"The baby?" He asked.

"Will be okay." I finished off for him.

He quickly took off his shirt and pants and threw them across the room and onto the floor.

"Lily, I can't think with everything going on right now." He said, stopping momentarily.

"Don't think." I replied quietly and put his manhood back in my mouth.

He sighed at me as I successfully managed to get him to focus on me as I stimulated him. He stopped me moments later and I climbed on top of him. I lowered myself carefully onto his manhood, biting my lip as I came to a sitting position on top of him. Although it was painful, I moved my body up and down, until I could move no more, sighing as I gave up. He rolled me onto my back and finished off.

"Wow!" He exclaimed loudly when he was done, sweat dripping from his face. "That was great."

I smiled nervously at him, as I pressed my body against his chest. I put my fingers to my lips. I didn't want his parents to hear us. He leaned over and kissed me hard and passionately for a few minutes before pulling away.

"I'm so lucky that you're my wife." He said to me as he pulled away, shaking his head in disbelief as he spoke.

"Yeah, you are." I replied, laughing.

"I'm serious." Antonio said. "I was completely stressed out and now at least, I feel some relief."

I smiled as I looked up at him. Curiosity overcame me. Did I want to know what was going on?

"You're the best." Antonio said.

I put my cheek to his chest for a moment, before pulling away.

"Antonio." I whispered. "I want to know what's going on. I want you to tell me everything."

Antonio sighed as he pulled away from me. He got up and went to the bathroom.

"Lily, it's nothing that you need to worry about." He said, as he climbed back into bed.

After looking into my eyes momentarily he turned around and went to sleep.

The next morning when I woke up, Antonio was in the backyard at his meeting and there were only two guards at the gates. I decided to confront Elena with what was going on when she came over and anxiously awaited her arrival. I woke up and went down to breakfast, feeling slightly upset after hours went by without a sign from her. She didn't get to the house until the men were out of their meeting and were ready to sit down to lunch. As we ate with them I tried to lead her off, but she excused herself immediately after lunch, saying that she had to take the girls to see the doctor. She said that she would be back later that afternoon, but I began to feel that she was avoiding me when she didn't show up.

Whatever was going on had to do with me, I decided as I sat quietly at the pool watching the nanny play with the twins. Now walking themselves, the boys were able to navigate around the pool and jumped in and out with their little life jackets on. As I sat there watching them I called Elena a number of times without any response. Carlos walked over to me a number of times to show me his hand as water dripped from it.

"Mira, Mira." He said, before happily jumping back into the pool after I nodded.

"What is going on?" I asked Roberta when she came over later that evening.

"What do you mean?" Roberta asked.

I immediately filled her in on my thoughts quickly and told her how I felt as if Elena was avoiding me. When I was finished speaking she laughed for a moment before letting out a deep sigh.

"Look, no one wants you to get upset." She responded after a moment. "You have the baby to think about."

"But Roberta, don't you see?" I responded angrily. "Not knowing what is going on is getting me more upset."

Roberta stared at me, lost in thought for a moment and then nervously looking around to make sure that we were alone.

"Liliana, you have nothing to worry about." Roberta finally responded. "You could actually benefit from what is going on, but for now it's not anything worth giving a second thought.

"Roberta, be honest with me." I responded, sighing as I spoke. Don't you think that the decision of knowing should ultimately be up to me?

I looked away from her momentarily.

"That man had a gun." I said quietly.

Roberta shook her head.

"No." She replied. "There is nothing to be concerned about. There is no way that he would have hurt you or anyone for that matter."

She glanced to the side and stopped talking as Antonio and Marcus approached. Antonio swooped down and lifted me to him carefully, kissing me on my lips nervously.

"What are you girls talking about?" Marcus asked Roberta.

She gave him an unconcerned expression, but said nothing. Antonio and her exchanged expressions and he immediately knew what was going on.

"Lily." Antonio exclaimed. "You have nothing to worry about."

I glanced from his face to Marcus's.

"I do, when it has to do with me?" I said.

No one said anything. Everyone exchanged glances that seemed to speak louder than words.

"Trust me." Antonio said. "No one around here is blaming you for what happened."

Marcus nodded and glanced over at me.

"I didn't say that they were blaming me." I muttered quietly.

No one seemed to hear me as I spoke. Roberta motioned at the house with her head and Antonio nodded.

"Anyhow, anyone in this town knows that if anything happens to my godson or his family, they're going to have me to deal with." Marcus said as he turned toward the house.

"Why would anyone blame me?" I asked again. "I don't get it."

"Enough with all of the questions already!" Roberta exclaimed loudly, motioning to Antonio and Marcus with her chin. "Let's go have some wine."

She walked quickly toward the house, Marcus and Antonio followed immediately while I stood in shock. I had never seen Roberta get so angry. What was it that everyone didn't want me to know? I glanced at the nanny and she nodded, as if to give permission for me to leave. I followed them in, a million other questions going through my mind as I walked.

The next two weeks were passed by slowly. I began to become annoyed with everyone around me. Everyone was being short with me, Antonio included. Elena was going out of her way to avoid talking to me and Roberta was much colder with me. I felt confused because I didn't know what was going on and didn't understand why everyone was so upset with me. No matter how much I tried to put the pieces together, they just didn't make fit.

Antonio had become apologetic with me, going out of his way to do things for me and to keep me busy so that I wouldn't begin asking questions. Although he didn't want me to ask questions about his business or what had happened, he did allow me to start doing some of his paperwork.

One day while Antonio was standing over me giving me numbers to put into the computer, Miguel came into the room and shot Antonio a disapproving glare. He sighed loudly as he stood in the doorway watching us to get Antonio's attention. Antonio lifted one eyebrow and Miguel immediately left the room. Antonio gave me the last numbers and said that he had to go down for his meeting.

When I didn't immediately follow, he grabbed my hand and suggested that I go have something to eat, pulling me out of the room with him. I couldn't help wondering what it was that he was hiding from me. Was there a possibility that I would find a clue that had to do with what everyone else already knew in his computer. As we walked downstairs, I pulled Antonio close to me.

"I want to know what's going on Antonio." I said sadly. "Why is everyone acting so differently with me?"

"What?" He asked, glancing away from me as he spoke. "No one's acting differently."

He pulled me close to him and I stood looking up at him, while I held him around his waist. I could barely reach his back, in the last two weeks my stomach had doubled in size. I shook my head and started crying. Antonio pulled my head to his chest and rubbed my back, letting out a sigh.

"What is it baby?" He asked.

"Everyone hates me." I said as I began to sob.

"No, that's not true." Antonio immediately responded as he rubbed my back.

"Yes it is." I replied. "Elena hasn't been over in almost two weeks and Roberta is acting differently with me."

"No baby, everything is fine." Antonio said, pulling me to our room and smiling. "No one hates you."

He opened the door of our room and glanced down the hallway. Miguel had gone back downstairs.

"Elena will be over later today, I promise you." He said as we entered our room.

He laid me on the bed as I whimper and lifted my dress to my waist. He lowered my hands to my sides and went down on me, removing my panties with his teeth.

"No, Antonio." I said. "I'm not in the mood right now."

He didn't pay attention to me as he slipped himself inside of me, working my body slowly until my tears were gone. I climaxed within seconds and he finished off minutes later. I lay still as he stood up and got dressed in front of me, smiling. I was fighting the urge to fall asleep. My eyes began to flutter and he came over to kiss them when he noticed. With the simple brush of his lips against my eyelids, I was knocked out. I slept until Elena walked into my room two hours later.

Luckily my dress was down, but my panties lay beside me on the bed as she walked into the room without knocking. I jumped up, grabbing my panties and rolling them in a ball as she came over and kissed my cheek. I was excited to see her, debating on whether or not to push the issue and ask what was going on. I ran to the bathroom to put my panties on, washing myself up a bit before coming out to sit alongside her on my bed. She smiled awkwardly at me.

"I should have called first." She said.

We both let out nervous laughs.

"Don't be silly." I replied. "Is everything alright? I feel like you've been ignoring me."

She smiled and touched my shoulder letting out a small sigh.

"Everything is fine." Elena said, unconvincingly.

As I looked at her with an excused expression, she stood up and walked over to our window.

"Come on. Let's go outside, the kids are all out there playing." I nodded as she wrapped her arm in mine and led me to the door.

As I walked outside, I noticed that Roberta and Marcus were there, playing with the kids. It was odd that they were both playing with the kids at the same time. It seemed as if Antonio had orchestrated the entire event to make me feel like everything was okay. Elena glanced over at Antonio and Miguel who were seated nearby in the yard, having a drink and watching us as we entered the playground area. Elena's expression as she looked at Antonio told me that she was withholding information from me, against her will.

I knew that everything had to do with what I talked to Antonio about that afternoon. I tried to go along with the act, but after an half an hour, I began to feel uncomfortable. I played with the twins until I grew tired and walked across the grass to sit down at the table with Antonio and Miguel. My stomach felt heavy and sweat began to drip from my hair because of the hot sun. Elena glanced over at the table as I sat down, but did not come to sit with us. Instead she motioned to Antonio and walked into the house. He glanced over at me, but I pretended that I hadn't seen her, focusing my attention on the twins. I glanced over at Miguel who sat typing a message on his cell phone as Antonio stood up.

Antonio bent over to kiss me on the top of my head, saying that he was going to go in to the house to get more ice for his drink and asked if I wanted anything. I shook my head and watched him walk through the grass, toward the house. I sat quietly for a moment before realizing this was the perfect eavesdropping opportunity. I glanced around at everyone and realized that I was the only one who had seen Elena motion for Antonio to go inside. I sighed loudly and Miguel looked up at me, as if just realizing that I was at the table.

"Oh gosh." I said, slowly standing up. "Antonio went to get more ice and I forgot to ask him to get me something to drink. Do you want something?"

"No sit down." Miguel said, standing up. "I'll get it."

I put my hand under my stomach, as if to show that I was uncomfortable.

"No, really it's okay." I said quickly. "I have to use the restroom."

I walked toward the house, glancing over my shoulder to assure that he wasn't following me. His phone beeped instantaneously and he looked down at it, quickly typing a response to whatever message that he had received. Marcus and Roberta were far enough away that they hadn't noticed Elena and Antonio go in to the house. I nodded at them as I walked in, signaling to them to show that I was going to use the restroom. I stopped at the door and quietly opened and closed it behind me.

As I walked into the kitchen, I stopped in my tracks. Not even three steps into the house, I could hear Antonio and Elena arguing.

"I can't continue to not tell her anything, Antonio." Elena exclaimed loudly. "She already thinks I'm avoiding her and I don't want to lie to her. You need to tell her."

"Not yet. Not until the baby is born." He responded. "We can't do anything to aggravate her condition."

"Antonio, I'm sure that she will be fine." Elena replied.

I could hear him slam his chair back and begin to pace the room. I knew that they were in the dining room and stepped back against to the door so that they wouldn't see me from the doorway.

"Really?" Antonio responded angrily. "Come on, think about it Elena. After hearing about this, we will be lucky if she wants anything to do with any of us."

Elena sighed and I heard him pull the chair back and collapse into the seat. He paused briefly.

"How could this have happened?" He said, lowering his voice as he spoke.

"It's a small world Antonio." Elena responded quietly. "It's not your fault."

I heard Elena walk over to comfort him. Antonio sighed loudly.

"It was totally my fault. I was young and stupid and needed to do what I did to protect you and my family." He responded. "I should have known that this would come back to haunt me."

"To haunt everyone." Elena replied. "Can you imagine what will happen if he becomes part of our lives?"

"Everyone else is going along with this Elena, why can't you?" Antonio responded.

"Because she's my friend." Elena replied. "My only real friend. I've known her longer than anyone else in the family and I don't want her to feel any more hurt than she's going to feel when she hears this."

Antonio didn't say anything. I imagined that he was sitting in his seat with his head resting in his hands.

"Antonio, this isn't your fault and it's not like you lied to her or held back any information from her." Elena said reassuringly. "You just found out. The sooner you tell her the better."

Antonio grunted, as if he was shaking his head.

"You just have to tell her and let her figure out how to deal with everything." Elena said. "She's going to be a mess, but she'll come around and we're all going to be there to support you when you tell her."

"When everything blows over, we'll have him to deal with." Antonio replied.

I put my hand to my chest and backed into the door. What was it that they weren't telling me, I wondered?

"Not until the baby is born." I heard Antonio say and stand up and begin walking in my direction.

"Antonio, you can't wait that long." Elena exclaimed as she raced to keep up with him.

I opened the door to pretend like I had just walked in from outside as he walked into the kitchen.

"Lily." He said, stopping as he walked into the room. "What's wrong, did you need something?"

I stood still without saying anything.

"I would have got it for you." He said, speaking very quickly. "How long have you been there?"

Elena came in after him and wiped a tissue to her face, as they both stood waiting for my answer.

"Oh, I just came in." I blurted out, trying to sound as believable as possible. "I was just going to pour myself some lemonade."

Antonio raised his eyebrow at me.

"It's so hot." I said dramatically, wiping my forehead as I stood in front of them, realizing the air conditioning and put a cease to my sweating.

They glanced at each other as I spoke. Elena pulled herself together immediately.

"Here, let me get it for you." Elena said as she went to the refrigerator and poured a glass of lemonade for me.

Antonio walked over to me and hugged me, kissing me lightly on the lips.

"Lily." He said quietly.

I nodded. Elena looked up, as if hoping that he finally had decided to tell me whatever it was that they had been talking about.

"I just love you so much." Antonio said. "You are the best thing that ever happened to me."

Elena looked down at my glass with a disappointed expression.

Just then Miguel called out to Antonio as he dashed in from outside. Antonio had left his cell phone on the table and missed a call. Antonio smiled nervously at Elena when he saw the phone number of the call that he had missed. She smiled back as she handed me the lemonade and raised her eyebrows, as if to tell him I told you so.

Antonio and Miguel quickly walked outside with the cell phone as Antonio proceeded to call the number back. While I was curious to know what Elena and Antonio were talking about, I decided not to press the issue any further. After hearing their side of the conversation, I knew that whatever it was, it was about me.

Elena and I walked outside and I sat down at the table with my lemonade while she walked over to play with the boys. I watched Antonio and Miguel as they stood just yards away from me. Antonio spoke silently into the phone and Miguel shook his head as Antonio spoke.

When Antonio was finished with his phone call, he put his arm around Miguel and told him whatever it was the call was about. Miguel raised his eyebrows and immediately walked over to Elena, Roberta, Marcus and the boys and began relaying the news quietly as well.

I sipped my lemonade and felt increasingly irritated as Antonio came to the table and sat down with me.

"What kind of business are you in?" I quickly asked.

Antonio leaned back in his seat and smiled effortlessly.

"A little late to be asking that, don't you think?" He jokingly asked, letting out a nervous laugh.

When my expression quickly went to a disturbed gaze he stopped laughing.

"One day I'll tell you." He said seriously.

The smile left his face, as he glanced over to the rest of the family. Elena sighed and ran her hand through her curly hair as Miguel filled the three adults in on the phone call.

Antonio and I sat silently as we watched the nanny come down for the twins and take them upstairs for their nap. Elena and Miguel waved as they left with their kids and Marcus gave Antonio a hand signal to call him. Antonio and I continued to sit silently at the table until he took my hand and led me up to bed, moments later.

When I awoke the next morning Antonio was already gone. It was bright outside, sunlight poured in through the wine colored curtains. I got out of bed and looked out the window. In one garden I could see that Antonio was having a meeting with a few more male family members than usual and joining them was a man that I didn't know, but who looked vaguely familiar to me. In the swimming pool area the nanny sat with the twins, watching them as they drank from their juice boxes. The man watched the boys with a smile on his face but didn't go near them. Antonio seemed uncomfortable as he sat with the man as they continued on with their discussion.

I tried to get a better glimpse of the man's face just as someone knocked at the door. Elena walked in happily, followed in by one of the maids carrying a tray of breakfast. I sat down on the bed and smiled as the maid left the room. Elena was smiling from ear to ear.

"Why are you so happy?" I asked while buttering my toast, quickly forgetting about the man.

"No reason." She said nonchalantly to me.

"Oh come on, tell me!" I exclaimed, covering my mouth as I stuffed it full of food.

She shook her head smiling.

"I'm not supposed to say anything." She said quickly.

"Now you have to tell me!" I exclaimed as I reached for my glass of orange juice.

"Who is that man, down there with the rest of the family?" I asked. "Does it have something to do with him?"

She suddenly looked horrified as I chewed my food. Her expression told me that I had nailed it. She shook her head and quickly turned away. After a minute, she stood up and walked over to my closet. I left my food and followed her as she walked in to it, wondering why she was acting so suspicious.

"Should I get dressed?" I asked.

She didn't say anything as she stood at my closet. I shook my head and went to shower and get dressed. When I came back to the closet after wrapping my hair in a towel I saw that she had started to put my clothes into a suitcase.

"Elena, what are you doing?" I questioned her.

She shook her head as she zipped up the suitcase.

"I can't say anything." She explained touching my shoulder as if to tell me to calm down. "I've been sworn to secrecy."

"What is it?" I asked again, in a more demanding tone this time as I sat down on the sofa in the closet.

She sighed and looked away.

"I can't talk to you about it." She said, gazing at me apologetically. "Antonio has to be the one to tell you."

She walked out of my room. I stood up and followed her to the stairway.

"Elena, what is it?" I called down to her.

She said nothing as she ran down the stairs and into the kitchen. Antonio and her nearly collided as he passed by her and ran up the stairs toward me.

"What is it?" He asked grabbing my hands.

I quickly pulled them away and ran back into our room, slamming the door behind me. I shook my head as I sat on my bed feeling confused. What was it that Antonio was hiding from me? Antonio opened the door to check on me as I lay in frustration. I felt my nostrils flare and pointed at the door to indicate that I wanted to be left alone. He reluctantly left the room without saying a word and I sat back on my bed, and folded my hands across my chest.

Antonio returned minutes later with Elena. They both entered the room, looking scared about what my response to them would be. I raised my eyebrows as they entered.

"Lily, so I thought that I should tell you that we are going to the States for a month." Antonio said lightly. "I will be taking care of some business and I that you could use a vacation."

I glanced over at the suitcase Elena had packed for me without saying a word.

"You guys are going to Chicago." Elena jumped in, bearing a forced smile on her face. "Isn't that exciting?"

I sat staring at them with a blank expression.

"How am I going to take care of the twins?" I asked. "Even with the nanny, I won't be able to run after them. Chicago is not like here, where they will have things to do and can run freely through the yard."

"My parents will be coming with us to help." Antonio immediately responded. "My dad is going to help me with the business dealings, and mommy will help with the boys."

"Your parents?" I asked.

"Yes." He replied. "My mother actually insisted on coming to help with the boys."

I glanced at Elena and she glanced away. The expression on her face told me that there was more to the story than Antonio was revealing to me.

"Don't worry." Antonio said quickly. "They will be staying in an apartment across the hall, so it's not like we'll be spending a lot of time with them."

This didn't help relieve any of my tension.

"How big is the apartment?" I asked, remembering my Aunt's tiny apartment. Antonio glanced at Elena.

Elena rolled her eyes and let out a sigh. Antonio walked across the room, making it obvious that he wanted to avoid the question. Elena shot me a glance from across the bed as she took a seat.

"You don't know?" Elena asked. "I thought you've been handling Antonio's paperwork, how did the apartment building get by you."

"Not all of it." Antonio said from across the room as he glanced out the window.

Elena focused on Antonio as he took a seat across the room in his armchair, facing us.

"Antonio you didn't tell her?" She asked.

Antonio shook his head and ran his hand through his curls while looking nervously out the window.

"It's not technically an apartment, or two that Antonio owns." Elena explained.

She glanced at Antonio and he shrugged, as if to give her permission to proceed to tell me the story.

"Antonio owns a condominium in Chicago." Elena continued. "The entire building."

Antonio sat nervously as he waited for my response.

"There are probably over a thousand condos in the building." Elena said without any empathy, rolling her eyes as she stared across the room at him.

"He should have told you about it." She went on. "He bought it some time ago. Even before you two met."

Antonio suddenly looked flustered as she stopped talking abruptly.

"More like inherited it." Antonio said uncomfortably.

"Before we met?" I asked Antonio immediately. "You never told me that you even visited Chicago."

Suddenly I felt very confused. I glanced across the room at the two of them.

"Why didn't you tell me that you owned a building there?" I muttered.

Antonio appeared to be flustered as I questioned him.

"I actually forgot about it until we began planning this trip." He said unconvincingly. "The money is deposited to my account and it's easy to forget about what comes from where."

He glanced away, as though he was speaking on a sensitive subject. I stared at him, feeling confused and annoyed as the puzzle grew larger.

"Everyone's coming to Chicago with us." Antonio said, attempting to change the subject. "I've arranged for the entire floor to be open while we're there."

I sat aghast, my mouth slightly open. We had been married for over four years. I couldn't believe that I was just finding out about this. I was beyond confused and though I had questions, I felt furry burning inside of me. Antonio and

Elena seemed to sense my frustration as I stared accusingly at them.

"You're going to love it." Antonio slowly continued.

I stared at him, feeling as if I was about to explode.

"The condo we're staying in is on the fourteenth floor of the building overlooking Lake Michigan." Antonio said as he stared at me blankly.

I raised my eyebrows at him. This was too much. What else didn't I know about him?

"I can't believe that you didn't tell me about this." I said quickly. "I don't care if the condo is overlooking the lake."

My hands began to shake as I sat before them. Elena quickly came to my side as I looked up at Antonio.

"I mean what else are you keeping from me?" I blurted out, stuttering as I spoke.

"I wasn't hiding anything." Antonio replied. "It just slipped my mind."

I paused for a moment as I stared at him.

"Who was that man that was with you at the meeting today?" I nonchalantly asked. "Why did you look nervous when you were speaking with him?"

I hit a nerve as Antonio immediately shot up, throwing his fist to the wall, though tapping it lightly. He passed the room and held his hand to his forehead as he glanced at Elena. She immediately shook her head and looked away. Neither of them said anything for at least a minute and Antonio seemed to be searching unsuccessfully for a way to get around the subject. His shoulders drooped, showing that he was ready to give up. As I sat watching them, I decided that it was time that I brought up the conversation that I had overheard long ago. Emotions ran through my body as I gathered my nerve.

"Tony." I said lightly, glancing from him to Elena. "I need you to answer something for me and I don't want you to lie to me."

He nodded at me nervously. I could see that fear was building between both him and Elena as if they both knew what I was about to ask. Elena sat on the bed next to me timidly.

"I don't want either of you to lie to me." I continued as I stared at each of them momentarily."

Elena sat up straight on the side of the bed and began to fiddle with her fingers. I could see her hold her breath in anticipation of what I was about to ask, but she nodded in agreement.

"What is it that I don't know about and that everyone is so scared that I'll find out?" I asked. "I overheard you both talking about it some time ago and you still haven't told me."

"What did you overhear?" Antonio asked.

"It's not important." I shot back. "Can you just tell me what it is?"

I climbed off the bed and walked across the room.

"I feel like there is so much that I don't know." I said lightly. "It makes me question our relationship."

"How can you say that, Lily?" Antonio asked.

He stood up and tried to hold my hand. I pulled my hand away from him immediately.

"Tell me." I ordered, but neither of them said anything.

"There cannot be any secrets between us, if we're going to work." I said.

I felt frustrated as I stood staring at him. Tears began to fall from my face as I became frustrated with their silence. Elena glanced at Antonio uncomfortably.

"Liliana, I agree that Antonio should tell you what is going on." Elena said carefully, stopping and glancing at Antonio momentarily before continuing.

"The thing is." Elena said as she paused, glancing over at Antonio.

Antonio nodded at her reluctantly to give her approval.

"I think that it would be best to discuss everything with everyone in the family present."

She stared at me as if she was examining my expression. I sighed in frustration, feeling that I would never find out.

"If we can wait till tonight, I'll make sure that he tells you everything." Elena said slowly. "We all will."

Antonio looked away from her, biting his lip as she spoke.

"Okay, tonight it is." Antonio replied in defeat, before quickly standing up and walking toward the door without looking back at me.

"Everyone is going to stay with me tonight because we are the closest to the airport." Elena said to me as she followed Antonio and held up her hand for him to wait for her when he glanced back at her.

"Besides, I still have some packing to do and we're going to have a big dinner tonight with all of our cousins before we leave." She said more to Antonio then to me. "The timing is actually perfect."

I nodded, sitting down reluctantly on the bed. It hurt me that Antonio was reluctant to tell me what was going on, and even more that everyone was withholding the same information from me.

"Sweetie, we have to get going." Antonio said, without directly looking at me.

"Wait, we're leaving tomorrow?" I asked, just realizing what it was that Elena was telling me.

Elena smiled lightly and nodded.

I had to trust that Elena packed everything that I needed and I wasn't sure how I felt about that. I didn't understand the rush to leave, as I followed Antonio and Elena out of the room. They were already at least five steps ahead of me and for the two of them to be walking through the house so quickly was unusual.

"What if we forgot something?" I asked as we went down the stairs. Antonio smiled and looked back at me.

"We'll buy another when we get there." He said nonchalantly. Antonio's attitude continued to surprise me. He was the type that had to make sure everything was in place before he did something. His actions as we prepared to leave the house scared me.

As we entered the dining room, the maid began bringing out food before we had even sat down. I glanced up at her nervously as I noticed the rushed expression on her face. I knew something was up, but Antonio and Elena did a good job of covering up their expressions as they sat before me.

Antonio Salvador and Blanca walked in just as the maid left the room, immediately going to prepare them a dish as well. Blanca shot Antonio an odd expression as the maid served her.

I glanced outside, where I saw the nanny playing with the twins at their swings. Moments later, I looked around the table and noticed that everyone was just about done with their food. I still had a full plate and began to eat faster. About five minutes later everyone was done with their food and watching intently for my last bite. Saved from their observation the nanny came in with the kids and everyone got up to greet them.

"Are you hungry?" Blanca asked Andres, who was visibly her favorite grandson. He shook his head and pointed at her drink. She immediately bent over to give him a sip, as Antonio complained to her about allowing him to drink from her glass. Antonio Senior smiled and beamed as he picked up Carlos. While he didn't seem to have a favorite, he was happiest when he held any of the grandkids. Everyone went out to the front and loaded into two limousines. The ride to Elena's house was a long uncomfortable one. No sooner did we pull up at Elena's house then Marcus and Roberta arrived.

"Sorry we missed lunch." She said as she hugged me.

Everyone walked into the house and quickly filed into the living room. I wondered what was going on and Antonio grabbed my hand, pulling me aside before I followed everyone else in, and kissed me deeply and passionately as Elena watched. When we pulled away, Elena walked toward me and brushed my hair from my face. Antonio continued on, passing the two of us and quickly was greeted by two of his cousins who continued on with him to the living room.

"How do you feel?" Elena quickly asked.

I nodded, as if to say I was okay.

"The baby? No problems?" She questioned me reluctantly as I shook my head.

I put my hands down at my side as she motioned for me to follow her into the living room. As we entered the living room there was a huge commotion going on. I hesitated as I stood in the doorway looking in at Antonio and his family. Elena walked into the room and took a seat next to Antonio.

"Lily, baby. Come in here." Antonio called out, when he saw me standing in the doorway. "There is something you've been waiting to hear, no?"

My heart skipped a beat as I walked into the room. Antonio Senior stood up and empathetically came to my side, leading me to the sofa and motioning for me to sit down before walking across the room to sit down next to his wife. Blanca had a horrified expression on her face and immediately attempted to leave the room.

"Mommy." Antonio said when he saw her. "Mom, come back here. I think you should be here for this."

Blanca did not turn around. She walked quickly out of the room and up the stairs, seconds later we heard a door upstairs slam closed. I glanced around the room and noticed everyone's serious faces. Antonio exchanged glances with Marcus and then looked over to his father for support, Antonio Salvador nodded.

"Lily, please sit down." Antonio said.

"What is it?" I asked as I reluctantly sat down next to him. Antonio sighed, exchanging worried glances with his father.

"What is it?" I asked, suddenly growing extremely nervous as I ran my fingers over the velvet material of the sofa cushion.

I glanced around the room and noted that everyone of any importance in the family was there, including several of Antonio's cousins that normally were not around us. My heart began to pound as I glanced around the room at them. Elena noticed my worried expression and walked across the room, sitting down next to me and putting her arm around my shoulders. The room grew so quiet that we would have heard a pin drop as we waited for Antonio to begin speaking.

"Lily, first of all," Antonio started as he glanced at Marcus for support. "Do you remember when Gilbert was shot a few weeks ago?"

I nodded and Elena rubbed my back as I wondered what that had to do with me.

"I have tried for years to protect you from the truth about what we do, or who we are for years." Antonio said standing up and beginning to pace the room. "Unfortunately it's come to a point where I can no longer hide everything or anything for that matter, from you."

He stood still as he stared at me, the curtains blowing quietly behind him.

"Unfortunately, you may be more a part of this than you would like to be." Antonio said slowly.

I nervously began to rub my stomach as the baby began to move from inside of me.

"You've asked me once or twice about what it is that I do." Antonio continued. "That is what my father and my business is."

Antonio smiled as he walked from one side of the room to the other.

"I mean, it's fairly obvious that we do not make our money running a coffee company." His cousins began to laugh lightly in the background.

"To be honest," Antonio said. "I'm glad that you didn't pressure of me coming clean with you before, but as Elena has mentioned to me, it is time that you know everything and my father and the rest of the family agree."

"Actually we don't have a way around not telling you this time." Antonio muttered as he began to pace the room again.

Silence went through the room as I stared intently at him.

"Liliana, I have to tell you something and you have to understand that I didn't realize this when I met you." He said quietly as he glanced at Elena.

She nodded at him and he looked away. The room was so silent that I swore I could hear my heart beating from within my chest.

"Ok, how do I start this off?" Antonio asked himself out loud. "Did you ever wonder why it was so easy for you to come here when you were younger?"

I stared at him blankly. I had no idea where this was going. I shrugged my shoulders at him as he watched my expression intently. I hadn't, although now that he pointed it out, I realized that everything did change for me very quickly after my mother was killed. I had always assumed that my paperwork had been rushed and suddenly I felt angry that he had brought it up. I could tell that Antonio noticed the change in my attitude and his expression immediately softened as he continued.

"Your mother lived here at one point of her life, not in our town but in one nearby." Antonio said slowly and glanced across the room at his father who nodded at him, encouraging him to continue.

I sat back against the sofa quietly, pushing Elena's hand away as she reached out for me. I had never known that and felt hurt that she had never shared it with me. I smiled lightly, more so in confusion than anything else as I waited to find out what else Antonio was about to tell me.

"This may be hard for you to comprehend, but she was engaged to a man that heads the cartel in Venezuela." Antonio went on.

My heart felt like it stopped between beats. I felt my hands begin to sweat and my eyes fluttered as he continued with the story. He couldn't be talking about my mother, he was obviously mistaken.

"Your father, or the man you believe to be your father was the man's second cousin." Antonio explained. "The man is known as "El Jefe. He is one of the scariest men that ever lived. She was afraid of him, but he was the one that brought her here. She left Venezuela with your father on her first opportunity without El Jefe's knowledge."

He sighed before continuing. Antonio's cousin's seemed surprised, as if they were hearing this part of the story for the first time. Some relief flowed through my veins. At least I wasn't the only one who didn't know the secrets pertaining to my life. Antonio glanced at me and I nodded at him to continue.

"At the time, your father was working for my cousin as a gardener. You were born in town and lived in my cousin's guest house with your parents for a couple of months, until "El Jefe" put two and two together and figured out that your mother had run off with his cousin." Antonio paused.

One of his cousins cleared his throat, as if he was choking on the facts that Antonio was laying out for us.

"Your mother insisted on fleeing the country when "El Jefe" came to town looking for her." Antonio said. "She made everyone swear not to tell him about the baby and she asked everyone in a way that caused there to be doubt in everyone's minds that you were your father's child."

My eyes got larger as he spoke to me. There was silence and my heart began to pound within my head, though I could hear every word that he was saying. I reached out and put my hand on Elena's knee. She reached down and squeezed it as Antonio continued.

"Your father went along with your mother and her wishes. He took his younger sister along and you all had to sneak into the country since Vito, or "El Jefe", had pretty much kidnapped her from El Salvador during the war and your father didn't have any papers." Antonio sighed before continuing. "After Vito began looking for your mother in Chicago your father got nervous and began abusing drugs. Eventually he was caught with a large amount of cocaine and served a few years before being deported back to Colombia."

Antonio stopped to look at me. I silently watched him as I let everything sink in.

"There's more." Elena said quietly and nodded to Antonio to continue the story. Antonio sighed and stared at me sadly.

"When your father came back here, he made contact with my cousin and asked him for help. He said that he needed to send your mother money to take care of you and to protect you from Vito." Antonio glanced across the room at his cousin who nodded in agreement.

"His commission as a gardener wouldn't cut it, so he began moving merchandise for us." Antonio said as I stared blankly at him. "He was moving cocaine for my uncle."

My heart pounded hard within my chest. I wanted to get up and run out of the room. Antonio sensed my shock and put his hand out in front of him.

"Our side of the family doesn't touch that stuff anymore." He said quickly in explanation.

His explanation didn't calm my nerves, my heart beat faster and faster in my chest, as he continued to explain everything to me. Elena clung to my hand tightly as if she could sense my anxiety.

"We didn't know that your father had a problem at the time and he and his girlfriend at the time, snorted so much cocaine that they both ended up in the hospital." Antonio said quickly.

"That is where we really got into the mix." Antonio said. "The man who shot Gilbert works for Vito. Actually he came back to the house again the other day. Vito ordered that we find out if you are his daughter and if the twins are his grandchildren. He has no other kids, so this is a big deal to him."

"A perfect reason for him to shoot Gilbert." Elena muttered under her breath, with a smirk on her face.

Antonio glared at her and she put her head down.

"The man that came to the house wanted to take you with him to meet with Vito, but didn't bother to explain the whole story to us and asked that we send you out to him or he would come in and get you himself." Antonio explained. "When we denied him access to the gate, he shot Gilbert. After I found out who was trying to get into contact with you, I called him. He explained the situation and I expressed my concerns as well. I let him know that you're pregnant and that this wasn't the right time to break the news to you."

Antonio paced the room before continuing.

"I took a glass that you drunk from to Vito and he sent it to a lab that immediately confirmed that you were his daughter. Vito instantly backed off, but wanted to see the kids." Antonio looked at me apologetically. "That was him at the house today."

I nodded and my hand began to shake with nervousness. I knew that I hadn't heard the worst yet. My beliefs were confirmed as Elena reached out and held my hand in both of hers. I looked down as Elena nudged me. I looked over at her, her eyes appeared apologetic. I remembered her being around several times before as I ate breakfast. I knew she had played a part in the test. Antonio studied my expression before continuing.

"The reason that we all worked with him is that Vito brought up a job that I had done for him a long time ago and threatened to tell you about it if I didn't cooperate with him." Antonio said. "So I did. I cooperated with him, the simple fact is, that he had us in a corner."

I shook my head as I stared at him. I tried to get up, but I was sunken deep into the sofa cushions. As he began to speak again, I removed my hand from Elena's and tried to cover my ears, afraid of what he was about to say.

Tears flooded my face as I sat completely still except for my trembling hands, which I held up to my face. He reached down and took both of my hands in his own, his eyes offering some explanation.

"Your mom." Antonio paused and sighed. "Your mom led her ex fiancé on after your dad was sent back home. She made him think that there was still a connection between them and maybe there was, but she never told him about you, he had heard rumors of the possibility of a child, which is why he continued to pursue her even when she was in the United States."

As I sat before him with tears streaming down my face, I realized that there was more.

"What was the job?" I whispered, shaking my head as if begging him not to tell me.

At first Antonio pretended that he didn't hear me. Elena began to rub my back in a circular motion, signaling to me that she was nervous about what was about to come. I stared across the room at the curtains that lay flat against the window as if all of the air had been sucked out of the room. I gathered my nerve and began to speak again.

"What was the job?" I asked, louder this time.

Antonio stared at me for a moment with fear in his eyes. As I studied his expression, I saw something that I hadn't before. I suddenly knew what was coming. I clutched my chest as he started to talk, hoping that what I saw was wrong, but knowing that I was ever so right. Tears streamed down my face and my shoulders dropped, sinking into my body.

"Lily, when your father tried to get away from Teresa, she was upset and told her cousin that was friends with Vito everything." Antonio continued. "Your father came to meet with my family for help. We knew Vito well. At the time there were a few things that we were working on for him. My father went to Vito and Vito told him what had to be done."

Antonio sighed in disbelief, as if he couldn't believe he was telling me the story. Elena nodded at him encouraging him to continue. I tried to pull my hand away from him, but he held it tighter as he looked at me.

"No one knew where your mother was until she bought a car." Antonio said lightly, choking as if he was about to break into tears himself.

Chills went through my body. I felt like everyone in the room had moved in a few steps and noticed that they were all focused on me. His cousins seemed to put two and two together and knew where the story was going. Everyone looked at me sympathetically as I turned away and put my head on Elena's shoulder. She immediately took my head in her hands and kissed my cheek, brushing my hair away from it.

"It was years later and I was in school at the time, near Chicago." Antonio said as he finally pulled his hand away from mine and leaned over, beginning to lower his head into it. "I was just beginning to express interest in getting into the family business."

I shook my head, I felt like I needed to get out of the room. I suddenly wanted to get as far away from everyone as possible. I began to stand up, but felt Elena's arm close around me, pulling me to sit alongside of her as I looked around the room in horror. I knew what was coming as I studied everyone's expressions. How could I have missed it, I asked myself? How could I have forgotten those eyes? I shook my head.

"No, don't tell me anymore." I said.

I glanced over at Antonio Salvador and he nodded sympathetically. As shocked as I was, I knew that I needed to hear it from Antonio. I knew that I needed Antonio to continue. I shook my head again. I felt glad that Antonio appeared to be hurt. I felt my heart turn to stone as Antonio began to speak. Antonio muttered something, but he spoke so quietly that I couldn't make out what he was saying.

A tear fell from my face as I waited for Antonio to pull himself together. I felt the pressure that Antonio must have felt right at that moment as I stared at him. Antonio become as nervous about what he was about to say as he looked in preparing to say it. He stood up and paced the room as he looked into the faces of his family members as he walked past them. Each of them nodded to him in support.

"What is it?" I murmured, grabbing his hand as he passed within inches of me. "Tell me."

Antonio stopped pacing and pulled over a chair positioning it directly in front of me. He sat down and looked deep into my eyes. He took my hands in his and held them for a minute without saying anything. I knew what he was about to say. I felt like I was melting as I sat before him.

"Lily." He finally said. "I killed your mother."

Book Club Discussion Guide
In Too Deep
by Neva Squires-Rodriguez

1. Is Liliana strong or weak? How so?

2. Antonio is different than what Liliana believed. How would you react to those things if you were Liliana?

3. The family treats Liliana in a variety of ways. Who do you think is the family member who treats Lilian best, and how so?

4. How did Liliana reconcile herself to her losses?

5. Elena was a friend to Liliana, as well as Antonio's sister. How did that friendship change?

6. How did Liliana's father support or not support his daughter in her trials and tribulations?

BONUS PREVIEW

Untitled

Book 3
The Liliana Series

by

Neva Squires-Rodriguez

Chapter One

I sat completely still for what felt like hours. I could hear Antonio's watch ticking slowly as he sat before me waiting for a response. What was I supposed to say? He had just finished telling me that he was the one who shot my mother. What was I supposed to say to anyone? I felt as if I was sitting in a room full of strangers. Even worse, I suddenly felt like I didn't know myself. I wanted to get up and storm out of the room, to get as far away from everyone as I possibly could, but I couldn't move. I felt like my body had frozen, as did everything else around me.

"Liliana, say something." I heard Elena say.

I sluggishly turned and gazed at Elena and the rest of the family without saying a word. Not a tear fell from my eyes as I sat staring at them. My eyelids blinked, notifying me that I was in fact awake. I turned very slowly and looked up at Antonio. His eyes appeared both apologetic and eager, as he waited for my response without saying a word. The truth was, I didn't know what my response would be. I needed direction that no one in the room was trustworthy enough to give me. I silently closed my eyes and lowered my head folding my hands in my lap and asked for direction from the only being I felt credible enough to guide me. I felt the hairs on my arms stand up as I felt the burn from everyone in the room watching me, but I needed direction. I did the only thing that I could think of doing and I prayed silently as the room full of Antonio's family watched me. I felt Elena put her hand on my shoulder, but I moved it away as I sat next to her.

When I opened my eyes, everyone stood before me frozen in time and waiting for my response. I felt surprised that my eyes were dry even though my chest felt like it had broken in half from beneath my ribs. Antonio and I stared deep into each other's eyes, me suddenly remembering every detail from the night that he shot and killed my mother. Gun shots echoed in my mind as one of the maids entered the room to see if anyone needed anything. Sensing the thinness in the air, she immediately went back to the kitchen. I shook my head to bring myself back to reality as I sat before Antonio and cleared my throat.

"I have to see him." I said silently.

"What?" Antonio asked, not hearing the words that I uttered from my mouth.

"I have to see my father." I said louder. "El Jefe."

A huge commotion immediately went through the room. Antonio's cousins instantly came to his side and began talking to him very quickly in Spanish. One began to yell directly at Antonio. Antonio tried to be calm, but within seconds, he was yelling back and all of the other cousins stood up to pull the two of them apart. Blanca came back downstairs and stood in the room with a distressed expression upon her face. She held her hand to her chest but said nothing as everyone watched the commotion go throughout the room as if it was a gigantic wave.

If I tried to understand what they were talking about, I'm sure that I could have. Instead my mind was elsewhere. I couldn't help but to replay the night that my mother died in my mind, the events repeating over and over. In some ways, I wanted to know what Antonio's family was saying. I wanted to see how much of my story they already knew in some ways, but at the same time, what I really wanted to do at this second was to talk to my father. I couldn't help thinking of the mysterious man that I watched, sitting down with Antonio in our backyard. The man that had eyed my children and smiled. Did he want to be a part of my life? Did he want to be a part of their lives?

I wasn't sure why I wanted to talk to this man that everyone hated so badly. I questioned myself as I sat there observing the intensity of the room, but the only thing that I could think of, was my father because I was certain that he was the only one who had the answers for all of the questions that I had. I began to wonder if he remembered my mother and what information he could give me about her. Surely a man like him had to have had at least a hundred relationships after her.

I glanced around the room and watched the people that I knew as my family fight and couldn't help feeling angry and hurt as I stared intently at them. I felt betrayed by everyone. How could they have known about what Antonio had done and expect me to be ok with it? How could they live with themselves, knowing what Antonio and the rest of his family did for a living? As I sat there watching them I realized that I also felt like I had betrayed my mother. How could I have laid down with the man that killed her? Why didn't I see the signs? Those eyes, that I had sworn so long ago that I would never forget, I didn't even recognize until now. A lone tear fell from my left eye as I sat as still as a stone sculpture and watched as everyone else in the room became lost in their own anger.

When the room finally fell quiet and Antonio's cousins stepped away, Antonio took my hands in his and looked me in the eye. I shook my head as I gazed up at him. I glanced around the room and noticed that everyone's attention was focused on the two of us. The burn from their glares was intense and I felt the heat as I quietly examined my surroundings. Blanca seemed to be full of regret as she watched us and Elena stood up and fell into Miguel's arms, quietly sobbing as if it would modify the situation.

"Did you hear what I just said?" He asked quietly. "I killed your mother."

The lone tear finally fell from my chin as Antonio sat studying my expression. He said the words slowly, as if that would make a difference. He said them in a way that made me feel like a child and suddenly I realized that before this moment I had been like a child to him. While we made love like husband and wife, he had always felt the need to protect me, neither of us realizing that it was himself that I needed protection from. I had been under his control and at his disposal and it made me angry. I felt my face begin to steam, my ears turn red and finally my heart turn to stone as I reached up and pushed the hair back from my face, allowing me to look him directly into the eye as I spoke.

"I heard you." I responded angrily. "Did you hear me? I want to see my father."

Antonio stepped back from me as if I had just slapped him in the face. My words had felt sharp as they left my mouth. I knew how powerful my response was to him and I knew that I had just disrespected him in front of his family. I couldn't begin to imagine what everyone must be thinking, but from their expressions, I had an idea. The fact is that every last one of them hated my father. I didn't have to know what was going on, to see this. I questioned myself as to whether or not they all hated me for same reason. I glanced quickly around the room, but then refocused my attention on Antonio. At this point he was my only concern, I would deal with the rest of them when I was good and ready.

Our gaze was instance. I could tell that Antonio was trying to contain his anger, as he literally appeared as if he was about to explode. Antonio cleared his throat and broke our gaze about a minute later, by turning around to contemplate the reaction of his family. I knew that he was wondering if they had caught my act of disobedience. He observed to their expressions to determine what move to make next, but when he saw the blank expression on some of their expressions, his gaze returned to me. I sat tall in my seat, I wasn't about to let him break me.

"Maybe we can arrange something when we come back from Chicago." Antonio said.

I shook my head. I knew that he had no idea how serious I was and I was determined to make him understand it.

"Lily, we can't miss this trip, it's a requirement." Antonio said convincingly. "The whole family is going."

Antonio glanced around the room for approval, before looking back at me.

"The tickets are non-refundable." He said under his breath.

"Then you go." I replied, as I smiled coyly. "I don't want to be around you or any member of your family right now."

"Are you kidding me?" Antonio responded. "Lily, I'm not leaving you by yourself."

"Then leave me with my father." I replied. "Or leave me at the house, the maids are there, we have security. I will be fine."

"Liliana," Antonio cut in, "Are you hearing yourself right now?"

I nodded him as I looked up at him as began to babble on. He was trying to convince me that I was making a bad decision. I knew that I very well might be making the wrong decision, but I decided that it was my place to decide that. I finally cut him off mid-sentence.

"Antonio, I'm not going with you." I said.

Elena gasped and the room fell silent. Everyone focused their attention on the two of us, more so than they had been focusing before.

"That's not going to happen." Antonio said. "I'm not leaving you here."

"You don't have a choice." I immediately responded.

How dare he, insist that I stay here with the rest of them, I thought to myself. How could he even imagine that this is something that I would be willing to do? I had to become my own person now. I needed this, I needed to know my father, if I was ever going to figure out anything about myself and who I was. Antonio stared at me for several minutes, as if I would suddenly change my mind. I finally shook my head and looked around the room, focusing my attention on each family member individually.

Blanca's eyes seemed to be full of sorrow. Her husband stood across the room without saying anything to her. Elena leaned against Miguel, as if without his support, she would fall over at any moment. When she noticed me focus my attention on her, Elena put her hand to her chest, as if my words hurt her. I couldn't take it. In my opinion they were all hypocrites. I forced myself to stand up and began to walk toward the door, still feeling as cold as stone.

"What about the boys?" Elena busted out, as I walked away.

I stood completely still for a moment before spinning around and shooting a glare at her that told her that this was not the time to question me.

"I need a break." I replied. "The world has come to the conclusion that I should know how to handle multiple devastations that are thrown my way. Call me a bad mother if you want, but I am going to sit this one out. I am going to leave the kids in Antonio's hands because he is their father."

I turned back, but before taking a step further, I looked back into her tearful eyes.

"I'm not a little girl anymore and I need to figure out what is important in my life."

"Liliana!" Antonio said forcefully, standing up and coming to my side. "I'm not allowing this, I have to put my foot down."

I laughed out loud, without recognizing what it was that was coming from within me. I glanced around the room as more laughter came from within me. It got to the point, where I was so confused with the sound, that it made me laugh harder and harder. My eyes began to water and I reached up and wiped my tears away, forcing myself to stop abruptly and to everyone else's horror I stopped laughing completely.

"You don't get it Antonio." I said. "You don't have a choice any more when it comes to my life. No one does, except me!"

With that I turned and walked out of the room. As I started up the stairs I heard footsteps run out to the hallway below me. I froze in the middle of the stairway, without turning back.

"Where are you going?" Antonio cried out after me. "We need to talk about this."

"I'm going to take a shower." I said without turning back to him. "I need to cool down."

With that I started up the stairs, ignoring the commotion that I had just created on the floor below me. I went to the room that Antonio and I always stayed in and closed the door behind me. I leaned back on it with my hands at my sides the moment I was inside as if it would protect me. I could feel my heart going a hundred beats per minute. For a moment I wasn't sure what to do, until I saw our suitcases on the floor by the foot of our bed. I opened my suitcase up, took my clothes out and went to take a steaming hot shower in an attempt to cool my nerves.

More Great Books by Neva Squires-Rodriguez

Liliana

by Neva Squires-Rodriguez

Book 1 of The Liliana Trilogy

Boom! That deafening sound changed Liliana's life forever. Her mother sits dead besides her, shot to death on the streets of Chicago. Within weeks, Liliana is sent to live with a father she doesn't know in Colombia. While working to pay off her father's debt, she meets the love of her life, who frees her from her father, only to bring her into a new world of twisted surprises.

Author Neva Squires-Rodriguez

Neva Squires-Rodriguez was born and raised in a neighborhood located on the North Side of Chicago. Mother, Wife, Expert at Multitasking... and now, Author, Neva creates electrifying stories with a twist.

Neva Squires-Rodriguez earned her Masters Degree from National University, a feat which she worked very hard to obtain and says she will work even harder to pay off.

She claims to be a typical American, full of dreams that will hopefully get her to a more comfortable lifestyle one day. She says, "God has a plan and I will follow wherever it is that He takes me."

Where to find Neva Squires-Rodriguez online

Website: http://NevaSquiresRodriguez.com

Twitter: @NevaRodriguez22

Facebook: https://www.facebook.com/pages/Neva-Squires-Rodriguez/1497271613835645

Blog: http://NevaSquiresRodriguez.com

www.ingramcontent.com/pod-product-compliance
Lightning Source LLC
Chambersburg PA
CBHW070831120626
46556CB00002B/720